THE MÉTIS PRINCESS

a novel by Annette Saint-Pierre

Pemmican Publications Inc.

Pemmican Publications Inc. gratefully acknowledges the assistance accorded to its
publishing program by the Manitoba Arts Council, Canada Arts Council and the Book
Publishing Industry Development Program.

Library and Archives Canada Cataloguing in Publication

Saint-Pierre, Annette, 1925-
[Sans bon sang. English]
The Métis Princess/ by Annette Saint-Pierre

Translation of: Sans bon sang.
ISBN 1-894717-27-9

I. Title. II. Title: Sans bon sang. English.

PS8587.A3493S3613 2004   C843'.54   C2004-907204-8

Author: Annette Saint-Pierre
Translators: Béatrice Tellie/ André de Repentigny
Cover and Book design: Kevin V. Forde
Cover Art: Marcel Durocher

He came back out, like an inquisitive child fearing a reprimand, and proffered a large oil painting. It showed a very young Martha, bright-eyed, with round dimpled cheeks and generous lips revealing sparkling white teeth. It was entitled: *A Metis Princess*.

One

The new graduate clutched his diploma nervously. Handing it to him, the president of the University of Winnipeg whispered, almost in confidence: "Good luck, Rôberre."

A half hour later, shoulders back, chest swelled with pride, the young graduate sang at the top of his lungs: *God Save the Queen*. In just a few minutes, he would sweep his mother into his arms, give his father a great big hug, shake hands with friends.

Robert was tall, a definite advantage for basketball and hockey, and no less an asset in the hallways of the university, where in the eyes of the female students, he stood apart as being neither timid nor snobbish. His presence seemed to spark witty remarks and anecdotes about provincial and federal politics.

In a group of Francophones, he didn't waste words in his criticism of Anglophones; on the other hand, his Francophone friends would have been astounded to hear him spin off on their own faults. Robert was not a hypocrite: he simply found it entertaining to make fun of the fears and foibles of both of Manitoba's founding peoples. He was serious enough: his own plans included a doctorate in history followed by a career in politics.

The processional moved forward. Black gowns, either too short or too long, traditional hoods lined in red, yellow, purple, white or green silk, mortarboards and headdresses in eccentric styles, fanciful creations of imaginative milliners. Some heads leaned forward, others were cocked to one side, still others were held high, daring and haughty; to Robert they were the receptacles of the great minds he admired. Getting an education to serve his people was the challenge he had set for himself ever since his formative years in the Scout movement.

The last notes of the organ recessional were followed by a cacophony of voices; here high pitched and excited, there nasal or hoarse, they rose and fell, buzzed and modulated in clumps of sound; Robert looked over one group after the other, searching for his family.

His feeling of elation was suddenly snuffed out; his stomach knotted with a strange foreboding.

"Robert, your parents had reserved seats. Did something come up?" asked a professor.

"I don't know. I left the house around seven to help hand out the cards to the graduates. My parents were ready to leave then."

"Take my keys. Let yourself into my office and phone home right away."

Later that evening, Robert burst into the entrance of Misericordia Hospital. He made his way through the long corridor to Emergency, not even pausing to apologize to the people he bumped into. When he saw Paulette and Jerome in each other's arms, he cried:

"Jérôme, what happened?"

"Dad's car was hit by a truck at the corner of Broadway and Smith. They've just taken Mother to another room for more tests, but Dad is still in emergency," was Jerome's explanation.

Jerome's wife, curled up in a sagging armchair, was trying to control her sobs in front of the visitors who had their own share of problems. Even though she was terrified of hospitals, she had come immediately, against her husband's advice.

Suddenly Paulette clutched her stomach; her moans brought the two brothers to her side.

"Excuse me," said a voice behind them. "Are you the children of Monsieur Lavallée's? I'm afraid I have sad news... but...This woman is about to give birth!" he cried as he noticed Paulette.

As Bernard Lavallée's life departed his body, another member came into the family. Jerome grieved his father's passing, at the same time rejoicing over his new-born child, who was bursting with life in the new mother's less than skillful hands. Death and life, occurring at once, were doubly shocking on a day carefully set aside to celebrate his brother's success. After all, Robert was the only one in the family to have gone to university. The banquet was forgotten, cards and gifts set aside, the champagne bottle unopened; they remembered the camera only a few days later at the funeral home.

They tried their best to put on a dignified funeral. The deceased left an empty bank account, and had fallen three months behind in his house payments. For two years, Bernard Lavallée had put all his savings into Robert's education. His widow would have to be thrifty and prudent in order to keep the family afloat.

In July, the mother accepted her fate; she would never walk again. From now on, she was confined to a wheelchair. They lowered the kitchen cupboards, increased accessibility to various rooms, installed bars here and there on the walls, and replaced the front steps with a ramp.

Jerome tried to convince his young brother to leave his mother in his care; as for Robert, the best arguments didn't hold when he considered the consequences of selling the house. What a dilemma! He would be free to study or to have friends over. But at what cost? His mother would lose her own freedom: she had made so many sacrifices for her son's comfort. Robert imagined his mother reduced to idleness in "her" bedroom or in some other part of Jerome's house, baby-sitting whenever Paulette asked her to. With his sister-in-law wanting to go back to work: live-in help would be only too handy.

Friends were siding with Jerome and Paulette, until Robert almost gave in, questioning whether his mother had the strength and perseverance to believe in herself and take charge of her life.

"Is it cruel of me to expect her to do things for herself?" he wondered.

One afternoon, returning home somewhat earlier than usual, he overheard his mother breaking off a telephone conversation. He realized she was hiding her tears. He was dying to know, but he respected her too much to spy on her. She was no ordinary mother! So strong and generous! Always ready to help! Forever alert to other people's needs! Sewing, knitting, cooking, cleaning, she took on so many tasks, never waiting to be asked. Everything about her was sympathy and understanding; even her voice revealed her deep and sincere love for all those around her.

If only Bernard was there... the house would once again be a haven of peace, her nights blessed with sleep and her mornings bathed in sunlight, under a roof that was the most faithful witness to their love. The night before the accident, Bernard had whispered in her ear:

"If I had to choose a wife, my love, I would choose you all over again."

He told her to rest, to enjoy life more, the boys no longer needed her so much. Lucille complied, neglecting certain useless chores to please the one she loved even more with each passing day. Later they hoped to travel, spend a few months at her sister's in B.C.

It hurt Robert to see his mother confined to a wheelchair. To draw her out of her lethargy, he decided to battle the odds. In the meantime, Lucille had devised one or two "tricks" to wash her hair. A long stick with strategically placed hooks allowed her to get cups and saucepans from the cupboard, to hang the clothes out on the line, to iron and fold; these minor victories gave her new life, made her feel useful. She was proud of her efforts, each day overcoming new obstacles.

"Aren't you going to ask who was on the phone?" asked Lucille, her dark eyes staring at Robert through a veil of tears.

"Seeing you crying, I don't suppose it was very funny."

"Jerome just announced he doesn't have time to mow the lawn, and Paulette can't do the shopping either."

"Oh well," Robert replied. "For people who seemed so eager to help out... Seems odd they would go on strike."

"They might be using this as an excuse to convince me to sell the house and go live with them..."

"What's got into them, I wonder?"

Robert took his mother's delicate hands and held them. She looked young and beautiful in her knit suit. Her flushed cheeks and anxious eyes spoke eloquently of the long struggle she waged from day to day. "Is there anyone who likes begging for assistance?" Robert wondered, as he silently observed the sick woman. And then how can you bear to be rejected? This time, however, Jerome's lame excuse had hurt Lucille Lavallée. No doubt about it, the elder son wanted once again to bring up the question of the family home.

"Mother, tell me, what do *you* want? Don't listen to what everybody else says. Just think of yourself for a minute. What would make you happy? Listen to me now: I want you to think of yourself. Where would you be most content?"

Lucille suddenly buried her head against her son's shoulder. Between sobs she blurted:

"I want to... stay... in my own house."

Two

It was not Jerome and Paulette's intention to make life difficult for their paralyzed mother; on the contrary, their invitation to live with them was meant to make her life easier and to free her of responsibilities. However, the thought of leaving the home where she had lived with her husband and children broke Lucille's heart. Robert and Jerome viewed the issue from opposite poles. Jerome saw his mother as a disabled woman, while Robert was convinced she would come out of it stronger than ever.

At the beginning of May, Robert started working at *The Tribune*. Every evening he spent an hour helping his mother with her exercises; then he took her out in the car, just anywhere: Henderson Highway, Wellington Crescent, Birds' Hill Park. He had other tasks too: today a fence needed painting, an eavestrough needed repairs; tomorrow he might loosen an old faucet or adjust a doorknob.

His friends started to worry when he stopped accepting their invitations. Robert had so many friends, he was exceptional in so many ways, forever the life of the party; how could he be totally indifferent to the sports and cultural activities he liked so much? A year had passed. Would he eventually come out of hiding?

"Shouldn't you think of yourself instead of organizing your life around your sick mother?" Brian said to him on many occasions. Robert had been so much a part of his life.

But his mother's condition was improving, and Robert hoped to see her walk again some day. His hope helped him forget the difficult task of nursing he had embarked upon. Feeling warmth and activity in his mother's legs as he massaged them, he put a blind trust in the optimism of the physiotherapist.

"Your mother's recovery depends on your determination and consistent efforts," she said.

"You can count on me."

"Is that a promise?"

"Absolutely!"

September was approaching, and Robert had plans for returning to school. Could he leave his mother alone? It was out of the question. Anyway, he didn't have enough saved up to pay for hired help in Winnipeg and live comfortably in Ottawa. He was determined not to touch a penny of his mother's pension. The thought had crossed his mind to ask Jerome for a few hundred dollars. But his brother had a wife and child... and his job as electrician wouldn't start paying good money for a few years yet.

"Robert, you haven't said anything about school," his mother remarked one day in the course of conversation. "You got another letter from the University of Ottawa yesterday."

"I've been thinking of the demands of a Master's degree and a teaching career... History doesn't appeal to me as much since I started at *The Tribune*. I think I'll open a night club in Winnipeg with topless dancers."

"Don't be silly! I want to talk seriously here. I've been thinking it over and I may have a solution."

Robert turned quickly. His mother was smiling. The previous day, he had taken her to a hairdresser who had coloured silver streaks in her dark hair. She thought she should have white hair "at her age," and she indulged herself from time to time.

"You look like a grand lady with your hair up."

"You're going overboard, but it's nice just the same," laughed Lucille.

"Okay, let's have your bright idea."

"Why don't we ask a lady companion to spend the night here? I wouldn't be alone, and you wouldn't worry."

"And what about in the daytime?"

"No problem. I have the phone."

"I'd still worry, so far away. Who would mow the lawn, shovel the driveway in winter, do the grocery shopping? And where will the money come from to pay this companion?"

"If I found the money, would you go to Ottawa?"

"Never! Mother, you can't even get up and walk without help. I'll go to Ottawa when you're walking in high heels... or if you take up bike riding, or dance the cha-cha."

Lucille's eyes filled with tears; her lip quivered. Robert just added more items to his list of wild ideas, and her tears changed to laughter. All right, she would prove to him she could get by on her own. She would stop trying to resign herself to her fate. From now on, she would do the stupid exercises the orthopedist had prescribed and she'd take them seriously.

No sooner awake, she stretched out on the bed and spent a half-hour performing the daily ritual. When she felt more courageous she took it a bit further: lying parallel to the back wall and pushing with both arms, she could roll over the other way, repeating the same manoeuvre a dozen times. The momentum in the turn obliged the limp legs to follow through.

Around ten o'clock, she lowered herself to the bare floor: With a broomstick she hoisted her legs onto the edge of the bed. On her back, legs elevated, she relaxed for a couple of minutes, and repeated the procedure: using her elbows, she pushed her body away from the bed, let her paralyzed limbs fall onto the rug, paused to catch her breath, inched close to the bed, grabbed the broom, lifted her legs, again, and again... determined to win at all cost.

At eleven, the neighbour who came to bathe her helped her to get up and into her chair. During the afternoon, Lucille put her legs on one or the other arm of the sofa. This exercise was more painful because of the pull on the muscles, with her thighs in a vertical position. She was aware of the risks... but inwardly, she knew she had to fight against herself and her inert limbs to make herself believe she could walk before September.

Robert didn't notice any physical changes, but he found her more cheerful, better able to concentrate on her reading and knitting, and spending more time at the piano. One evening, she handed him a note from Social Services:

"I have the address of a sixteen-year-old girl who wants to live in a home in exchange for household chores. This could be the break we're looking for. She's willing to work for room and board. But I could give her some money. After all, we can't take advantage of her."

"Is she pretty?" joked Robert. He felt this Martha Star would be more trouble than she was worth.

"Robert, please be serious; don't write this off without giving it some thought."

"Do you want me to go with you to the interview?"

"Yes," Lucille answered firmly. "You know what I'm thinking? If she comes to stay with me, you can go to Ottawa."

"We'll see," Robert answered off-handedly.

The trip took them across the Norwood Bridge, and onto Main Street, past the majestic CN station, the tall Grain Exchange Building, the Bank of Montreal and the Westin Hotel; further on was the handsome Centennial Concert Hall, and the splendid Museum of Man and Nature.

Beyond the railway bridge, the scenery changed totally. With dismay, Lucille observed a different world: Winnipeg's poor. Row upon row of run-down smoke-blackened buildings. Brave as she was, Lucille was suddenly overcome with shame; she felt out of place, wondering if people were pointing at her. In the filthy streets, pedestrians shuffled on, as if sleep-walking, living examples of intellectual and moral deprivation. The rich never set foot here.

Robert knew Manitoba history; he told his mother the majority of immigrants from central Europe were first housed in this part of Winnipeg, without water or sanitation. After an alarming death rate from typhoid fever, TB and scarlet fever, the authorities stopped sending people to this unfortunate "dump." Gradually, the first residents were able to leave "North Main" for more desirable neighbourhoods. Later, however, Natives who had left their reserves found homes in this district where rents were more affordable.

Lucille Lavallée was aghast. From both sides of the street, she was assailed with scenes of poverty and degradation. An old man, standing on the edge of the sidewalk, urinated into the sewer. Three youths accosted a little girl of eight or ten and enticed her into a back lane. An old woman was searching through a garbage can. Two heads hidden under long manes, young mouths joined together, the boy's hands groping under the girl's panties. People staggering out of taverns, loitering on street corners and under the marquees of run-down movie houses advertising lowbrow films. It was surprisingly still. The Indians and Métis seldom speak; when they do, their voices are sweet and thoughtful.

Lucille Lavallée had seen Natives in waiting rooms of bus stations or in department store entrances, but she had never set foot in such a ghetto. Robert stressed that the city of Winnipeg was trying to restore certain buildings and create green spaces, but they had to negotiate with a "race" who had privileges and rights to its ancestral territory.

Policemen were present in this Main Street district: on foot, on motorcycles or in cars. Nevertheless, thefts, brawls, rapes and murders were daily occurrences among these unemployed people, better accustomed to hunting and fishing. What can an itinerant hope to achieve in Winnipeg? What employer would risk hiring an Indian of questionable reputation?

Young people who had attended the White man's school knew that there was a double standard; television sent them images of how society saw them. A few were convinced they must change environment in order to stop being the dregs of the White man's society. They envied the white man's standard of living, and wanted to leave Main Street as soon as possible. To go where? No one knew. They realized it was a mistake to have left the reserve. Would they make another mistake by renouncing their ties with the Indian world? Were they condemned to be forever treated with contempt?

"Poor girl! How can she even go out alone?" wondered Lucille, thinking of Martha Star.

Meanwhile, Robert's attention was drawn to a scene on the sidewalk.

"It looks like she's broken her back."

"The other one has only one leg. How awful!"

Robert was distraught. Every time he drove through this neighbourhood, he reflected on the responsibility of Whites. He had once written a paper on the living conditions of the Indians, and done some research for a documentary with an Anglophone student studying the same question.

"Two solitudes," he commented. "Here we are. The servant of your dreams lives above this grocery store. I'll lock the doors and go for her. Wait here and don't talk to anyone, even if they seem desperate. If something happens, blow the horn three times, and I'll come down at once."

The railing was sticky and the stairs spattered with fresh vomit. Obscene graffiti on the walls reflected the degree of morality of the owner and tenants.

"A bit of paint wouldn't be a luxury in this dump," Robert muttered. He was quite certain he had come all this way for nothing.

On the fourth floor, the door numbered 431B was ajar. Inside, he saw rickety furniture, cracks in the plaster walls, and cupboards practically stripped of paint. But it looked clean and even smelled of a recent soap and water scrubbing. He heard whispering from somewhere inside. He was not expected, so he knocked again. A few moments later, a woman in her thirties appeared, carrying a basin and a towel. She was White!

"Good evening, Madame. Are you Martha Star's mother?"

"Yes," she replied rather timidly. "Sit down, Monsieur."

"Thank you. I've come to meet Martha and to introduce her to my mother. My mother is handicapped and couldn't come up."

"Martha... Well. Martha is sick. She fainted a few minutes ago so she can't make it downstairs. Can you come back tomorrow?"

"Yes, of course. Tomorrow, same time," said Robert. The woman appeared to be a decent person, and the girl behind the door rather delicate."

"Come back at the same time. But please come back," she pleaded. "Don't forget. Martha would be so disappointed, and so would I."

The trembling voice followed him down the stairs:

"Sorry! We're so sorry!"

Madame Lavallée was disappointed, but Robert reassured her.

Secretly Robert wondered about this well-mannered French-Canadian woman living in the North of Main Street. If the father is White, he concluded, Martha is neither Indian nor Métis.

Three

Martha's mother, Gisèle Bergevin, was born in Québec. One summer day, a missionary from Western Canada had brought a group of Native singers and dancers on tour to several villages. The shows had attracted young people, especially girls who found the Indians "cute" with their black hair, white teeth and coffee complexions.

The Manitoba musicians weren't "real redskins," rather, talented and charming young men. They were students at an Indian school; Oblate fathers ran the boys' section, and the Oblate sisters looked after the girls. At Saint-Eugène, Gisèle had fallen for the guitarist, Norman Star; she was so taken by him that she tried to see him again.

After a few meetings, she was convinced Norman was every bit as nice as White boys. He was twenty, and had just finished grade twelve; he planned to register in a Winnipeg community college. He swore eternal love in a song to his White princess. On the eve of his departure as he repeated his marriage proposal, he shed a tear: he would die if he couldn't see her again. He even suggested she follow him immediately.

Charmed, Gisèle was tempted to board a train for Winnipeg without telling a soul; fortunately, she hadn't completely gone out of her mind, and asked the group leader for advice. Father Letendre's reply was unequivocal.

"Absolutely not. Don't ever be so foolish. You're only sixteen years old, and marriage is a commitment restricted to adults, not adolescents. I certainly hope your parents agree with me."

"They don't know anything about it yet."

"So much the better! They'd go crazy if they found out. Go on with your life; in time you'll forget about Norman. White girls don't marry Indians."

Norman left, dragging his feet, a look of defeat on his face. But each day during the Québec tour, he wrote her letters full of promises. He was as talented for drawing as he was for music: his letters were adorned with emotionally laden sketches. He labelled them: "Gisèle on the beach at lake Winnipeg, Gisèle in a canoe on Lake Winnipeg, Gisèle getting off the train at Winnipeg Station, Gisèle on horse back, Gisèle watering the flowers in her garden, Gisèle in Norman's arms, Gisèle holding her first child." In a state of euphoria, the naïve teenager told no one of the plan developing in her silly head. She ate little and spent more and more time alone, happy to dream her life away rather than living it.

Between the walls expressing Norman's faithful love, Gisèle spent all her time reading or writing love letters. Her mother had noticed the strange display that had cropped up magically, but she didn't pay too much attention, busy as she was looking after the family. During that period, her daughter sought refuge in her imaginary world where she lived in a castle inhabited by a prince. The lover who filled her dreams and daydreams was unique in the world; she idealized him more and more, and saw faraway Manitoba as a land of milk and honey in an unknown world.

In September when Norman begged her to come to Winnipeg, Gisèle finally got up enough courage to tell her parents her secret about the missionary's guitarist who had visited the Bergevins in their home. Her revelation met with a harsh and uncompromising reaction:

"If you marry an Indian don't ever set foot in this house again. And if you get into trouble, we don't want to hear about it."

Norman bewitched her with words of love, destroying her last defences. What was there to fear? Wouldn't he be there to protect her, to love her, to make her happy? In Winnipeg, life would be rosy. Norman had started a mechanic's course, and found a part-time job. Everything was falling into place.

A month later, Gisèle boarded the train for Winnipeg. "Finding" the money for the fare had been too easy. Monsieur Bergevin was in the habit of keeping a roll of bills in his pockets and of leaving the money when he changed his trousers. Mischief was not new to Gisèle and pinching the money had been an easy matter. Nonetheless this first dishonest gesture was to haunt her during the long exhausting trip. Pine trees as far as the eye could see... rocky terrain... isolated cabins along lakes and ponds...

Winnipeg! At last! Gisèle was so happy to see Norman again. She was certain of her decision. Alone with Norman in a big city! No one knew them. What a contrast with the atmosphere of a little village where you can't cross the street without the whole town knowing! Norman lived at the Winnipeg Indian Residence. He had assured her the nuns would be happy to take her in for a while; but the night of her arrival, to Gisèle's surprise, the oh-so-perfect fiancé had other plans.

"Gisèle, don't you understand. We have to celebrate your arrival. We have so much to talk about. It's just great to be together at last! We'll go to the residence tomorrow."

"But... I don't want to..."

He was leading her towards the entrance of the Aberdeen Hotel, near the restaurant where they had just eaten a meal of tasteless spaghetti. Gisèle begged him not to insist, trying to free herself; but he was strong, and she was unable to resist him. He was panting and perspiring profusely. She felt ashamed seeing the hotel clerk had guessed his customer's intentions. The poor girl looked away, attempting to free herself from the man who gripped her tightly around her slim waist.

Their first passionate love-making was so disappointing, in a grimy, squeaky bed, grey curtains flapping. The tiny window let in humid air and unpleasant noises. The "great" lover slept like a log till morning; the princess beside him lay awake, counting the hours and following the minute hand on her watch. She was crying. Angry, but not desperate, she promised herself she would change this boy; she would teach him manners; in short, she would transform him into a gentleman like her father. Naive and gullible, she dreamed of a better tomorrow.

Gisèle saw Norman every day at the Academy Road Residence. It was there she became friends with the nun in charge of the girls. During her twenty years of service, she had seen it all in this unique, closed institution. She had witnessed many affairs and break-ups between Whites and Indian girls. However, she believed Norman was the first to dare propose marriage to a White girl.

"Why don't Indians marry White girls?" she asked Sister Bernadette.

"They don't often get to know White girls. Anyway we have to wonder if an Indian who hasn't had White male models would know how to treat a White woman. I suppose an Indian behaves towards his wife just like his father treated his mother. Usually, an Indian girl is happy to marry a White man who brings home a regular pay-check. I'm not saying Whites are paragons of perfection, but the majority of marriages between White men and Indian women work out reasonably well."

"I'm sure I can change Norman if I marry him."

"It's not easy to change other people, Gisèle. You'd do well to accept him the way he is, and that's how he's going to stay."

"If Indian girls adapt to White ways, why couldn't Indian men do the same? The cook here, Madame Labonté, is an Indian married to a White man and they both seem happy."

"Did you know that Indian girls spend about ten years in residence with the nuns? They learn to keep house, to dress elegantly; after they're married, there's nothing to stop them from maintaining the same life style. It seems we unintentionally prepare them for marriage to White men."

"Why don't you prepare boys the same as girls?"

"It's so different. They stay in contact with other Indians, educated or not, continue to fish and hunt, go off in the wilderness, or loaf and drink together. More often than not, they're unemployed; they get discouraged and lose all ambition; in their frustration, they blame White men for their failure. That's why a White woman risks becoming the scapegoat. Just an example: Indians really reject the White man's society. When an institution closes, which was part of their childhood, they vandalize the building. They smash windows and break down doors, their anger directed at the symbols of their alienation."

"Norman is so nice to me. He's doing well in school. He likes his job. I trust him. I love him."

"Norman will have to change environment if he wants to adopt the White man's ways; otherwise, he'll go back to his people. Gisèle, would you be prepared to live like an Indian?"

"Never! Can you imagine, Sister? I'd be like a fish out of water," Gisèle replied. She had noticed the look of discouragement on the faces of Indian women she met in the streets of the city.

"Well, in that case, you'd better find out what Norman is planning for you before you promise to marry him," Sister Bernadette warned gently. "If he decides to return to the Fort Alexander Reserve, you'll have to go along, and you might feel lost over there. You're just a child, and you're about to sacrifice your youth to situations for which you have no preparation. If I were you I'd go back to Québec and I'd think this over very carefully. You'd be wise to invite Norman to go and join you and to adapt to the life you choose for him."

"I'm sure I'll never love anyone else."

"Poor girl! You wouldn't buy a new coat before trying on at least ten; you'd even go to several stores to find the one best suited to your age, your style and your pocketbook. Think about it, Gisèle. Don't you understand you should be at least as cautious about choosing your companion for life? A husband is rather more important than a coat, and you're blind... you're fooling yourself."

The last argument had the desired effect on Gisèle. She took her time buying dresses and sweaters; selecting a coat was a major production. She promised to think it over seriously before giving Norman a definite answer.

Five days later, the young girl learned she was pregnant. She cried for days.

Four

They were married one sunny morning in November, in the chapel of the Fort Alexander Indian Reserve, about a hundred miles north of Winnipeg. The white gown was a gift from Father Letendre himself; as he considered her delicate body, he thought her chances of happiness were equally fragile. While the couple exchanged vows, the missionary was distressed by an onslaught of sad images. Norman wasn't a bad person... just too much of a dreamer and too optimistic with his White princess on his arm.

It was the groom's wish that no Indian rites be observed by the residents of the reserve during the festivities following the ceremony. The rickety benches were already occupied when the young couple entered to the sound of an orchestra. No feathers to recall Indian traditions, rather streamers and paper flowers; no address by the chief, no symbolic tribal gesture, instead Elvis-Presley-type songs speaking of love.

"Come and dance!" they cried over deafening music, or to fill the embarrassing silence at the end of a selection.

Ignoring their native dances—including the sacred ones—the spectators stayed in their seats, hesitant to perform the latest gyrations learned "outside the boundaries." The Saulteux elders hung their heads, anxious and ill-at-ease; the celebration made no sense to them. Gisèle, seated on a rustic bench, held Norman's hand. Suddenly she got up and led her partner onto the dance floor: two bodies moved as one, two hearts beat to one rhythm. The astonished guests showed varied reactions as they watched the gracious white figures moving around the dance floor: the young envied Norman's White ways; the old people stared at the toes of their rough shoes: What of the future of the race? Our customs?

Our traditions? Our language? Another one is starting a family, but joins the ranks of the Whites.

Norman was handsome: a full head of hair, dark skin, and bewitching eyes—the alchemy of maleness, he had ravished a girl who said she was going back to Québec. An upsetting letter had made her hesitate at the last minute: she could come home without fear, as they promised to forget she had run away to the Indians. But she could not resist Norman's warm kisses and passionate caresses, the bright lights of Winnipeg, and of course, the sweet taste of freedom.

The baby was born in July in the Winnipeg residence; she was christened Martha Bernadette; Martha for her maternal grandmother, and Bernadette for the nun Gisèle liked so much. But the dream of a home in the big city disappeared in the cloud darkening the young couple's future.

The August sun burned the crops and tortured city-dwellers. The couple couldn't resist leaving their miserable two-room apartment for the fresh air of Lake Winnipeg. There the lake harboured their illusions and cast a renewed spell on the reserve.

"Why couldn't we live in Pine Falls?" asked Gisèle, one day. They were on their way back to Winnipeg after a weekend at the lake.

Norman was silent. Why revive the anger he had felt when he had brought up the matter with his parents years before? The Abitibi Paper Company owned all the houses in the town of Pine Falls and they wouldn't rent the poorest shack—if there was one—to a "dirty Indian."

In September Father Letendre hired Norman to spare him the hardships of unemployment and poverty in Winnipeg, but most of all because he pitied "the little French girl." When the young family arrived, the employees organized a bee to paint the house, the nuns polished the windows and put up curtains in the "palace"—what the Indian women called the White woman's house. After all, she had a lamp in the window and flower pots on the porch.

From now on, Gisèle would live in an Indian environment. If only her parents, and brothers and sisters could see her now! She was happy—for a while. One day her husband left his job to go trapping with a few buddies of questionable character. The three nights she was alone, she was afraid: someone tapped on her bedroom window. When he returned, Norman examined the footprints in the snow. Encouraged by his buddies, he went off to follow the suspect, a White man from Pine Falls who visited Indian women when their husbands were away. The desire for revenge fuelled his anger.

They had it out behind the Manitou Hotel. Norman was so drunk he could hardly stand up. The stabbing he inflicted was not fatal but earned him four months in jail. Father Letendre was devastated! He tried so hard to make men out of "his" Indians... and the one who showed most promise was no better than the rest. He could count on one hand the boys he had educated. Norman was the one he used as an example of success whenever his colleagues were ready to give up. You could be optimistic as long as the Indians, male or female, lived in the residence, but left to their own devices, they soon succumbed to their native ways.

Gisèle, sad and disillusioned at Norman's behaviour, returned to the Winnipeg residence; the superior put her in charge of the sewing workshop. She managed to save some money, fearful of a bleak future. Two weeks after the prisoner's release, the young family moved to Winnipeg, near the residence, so Gisèle could keep her job with Sister Bernadette. Even though she spoke English fluently, she felt nervous and helpless in the White man's world; she was more comfortable with her Indian neighbours. They quietly showed their friendship by helping her whenever she was in need. At seventeen, a stranger among both Indians and Whites, Gisèle anguished over her future. What kind of life would she have in Manitoba?

Norman worked in a garage for four years, thanks to the brother-in-law of an Oblate father's, who ignored the lateness and absenteeism. Unfortunately, a new owner, who did not feel obliged to the Oblates, and much less to Norman Star, fired him after two or three warnings. The Indian had become a regular in the Main Street bars frequented by his buddies, but Lady Luck smiled again. Father Chartrand, superior of the Winnipeg Indian residence, hired him to supervise the boys.

Gisèle asked Sister Bernadette to have a word with the superior to let them live on the third floor of the huge building set in a forest of willows, mountain ash, and Chinese elms. Little Martha was everyone's sweetheart; as soon as she came into the game room, they picked her up, tossed her about, like a big rubber ball, catching her "on the fly" while she shrieked with delight. This went on until she got tired and started to whine.

Martha was now of school age, and it appeared she would have to go to English school. Norman couldn't see the problem: in the residence, no one spoke French. But Gisèle had gone to convent school in Québec, and wanted her daughter to attend a similar school to learn French. As the cost was prohibitive, Gisèle spoke to Sister Bernadette about her financial situation.

"No, keep your money," said the sister. "I'll speak to the superior of the Lorette convent; they take needy children there. They don't broadcast it, but I tell you they often take pupils who can't pay. I myself was a boarder in a convent and never paid a cent."

"I could help out by cleaning for them."

"Poor Gisèle. You don't have the strength. Three miscarriages in two years! I wonder if you might be anaemic. There, there, don't cry. Here, wipe your tears," said the sister, handing her a tissue she produced from a drawer. "Does Norman drink a lot?"

"Not really. But he hates spending his time imposing rules he wouldn't obey himself. He says Native children are born to be free, and that they reject the White man's discipline as stupid and unbearable."

"Are you happy, Gisèle?" asked Sister Bernadette in a whisper.

"Yes and no. It's hard to say."

"Do you regret your marriage? You were so unsure. Do you remember?"

"Norman is good to me. But things are different now; the little one is growing and I'm worried. If she spends her whole life with Indians, she'll end up believing she's one of them. She'll end up like me—a stranger among White women."

"But you still haven't answered my question. Are you sorry you married Norman?"

"I think so. You were right, Sister, to advise me to go back home even though I was pregnant. But would my parents have accepted Martha? And my sisters! They're such snobs, they would have disowned me, and I would have been an embarrassment to the family. If I must hide, I'd just as soon hide here in Manitoba."

Martha was sent to the Lorette convent and went to elementary school there. At fourteen, she continued on to high school. As her parents lived in the Winnipeg residence, she could spend summer and Christmas holidays with them. She was a bright girl and soon mastered both French and English, although she was obviously timid in normal conversations. The Lorette girls thought she was "right out of the woods." The first time she had had to reveal her nationality, she got up and declared:

"I am Indian."

Uncomfortable with this announcement, the teacher explained to the class that Martha wasn't pure Indian, seeing her mother was White: only her father was Indian! Conscious of the wave of whispering all around her, Martha realized she had committed a faux pas. Saddened, she kept to herself, avoiding the girls who had made fun of her behind her back, and even more so the sister she had displeased. During the next vacation, she brought up the topic with her mother, whose confused explanation convinced her she was a member of an inferior race.

The day of reckoning had arrived! How could Gisèle make her daughter accept a nationality which was a constant source of humiliation? Neither White nor Indian, the Métis belonged nowhere. On the one side, the Indians scorned them; on the other, the Whites avoided contact with a people they considered a bastardized race. There was only one solution: assimilation with Whites.

Following her conversation with her mother, Martha anguished over her identity, and became increasingly silent and solitary. The mother had failed to find the right words to explain to Martha how to accept her fate, and the daughter became more and more introverted. At school, if someone spoke to her, she answered politely but timidly: only Sister Hélène could get a few words out of her when she went for her music lesson.

One day, Sister Bernadette had praised the Métis "nation." Martha was quite taken by the exploits of her ancestors: the Saulteux buffalo hunters who prayed to the great Kichi-Manitou, the master of life and creator of the world. More and more, she wondered why her mother pushed her to be White, and no longer spoke of her Métis origins.

The Indian residence closed down when the federal government changed its policy regarding integration. The religious orders left Winnipeg for good. Unemployed, Norman and Gisèle went to live in a tenement on Main Street; Martha would live with them when she finished grade ten. She was shocked to see her mother so depressed! And her father seemed to spend his life in a silent stupor! Was he alcoholic? Were they discouraged? Sick, perhaps? She didn't understand.

Sister Bernadette had advised the mother to simply give Martha their new address. In the meantime, aware that the young Métis was facing more trauma when she returned home, Sister Superior watched her closely. The eve of her departure, she called her to her office and asked her to return in September, free of charge, to take grade eleven. Could she manage without the nuns' generosity? Martha almost agreed, but finally, she asked to think it over for a few weeks. What could she do instead? Where would she go? During the course of the last semester, she had obtained high marks, and so she wanted to pursue her studies. Furthermore, she had friends among the boarders; she was friendly and always willing to help. She was a talented musician, and had taken part in recitals and played the organ at church services.

In high school, there were at least a dozen ethnic groups represented, so the topic never came up; there was a climate of mutual trust and respect among staff and students.

"Martha, who would know you're Métis?" commented the physical education leader one day.

"What would be different if you did?" asked Martha.

The young man didn't answer.

"Would you put me down?" retorted Martha.

"No, not put down..."

"Not put down, just cast aside. Say it..."

"Look, Martha, I've been watching you for a while. The other students like you and enjoy your company. But... aren't you interested in boys your own age? Why do you hold back? Every time a boy pays attention to you, you avoid him. It's obvious."

"I'm shy," she confessed. She spoke more quietly now. "Because they look at me strangely. You know I'm Métis, and... different from White girls..."

"Not at all. Make me happy. Let me drive you to Winnipeg on the last day of school."

Martha almost passed out when she saw 731 Main Street. She was burning with shame; she felt herself blushing from head to toe; the smell of garbage sat on her skin; the barks of a ravenous dog churned her stomach. If she had known where her parents lived, she would have refused Laurent Thibodeau's offer. Why had she imagined they lived in a pretty little house? Thibodeau, floored by so much ugliness, took Martha's suitcase upstairs and forgot to say hello to Mrs. Star. He clambered down the steps as fast as he could, as though he had mad dogs at his tail.

Martha fell into her mother's arms, sobbing and gnashing her teeth. She felt only disappointment, distress and despair. Was this real? Her student world had fallen apart. Gisèle was distraught: she felt responsible for her daughter's pain.

Five

Gisèle sat at Martha's bedside, bathing her forehead with a cool towel. She tried to be cheerful as she announced a distinguished gentleman would pay them a visit the following day.

Martha's illness was not serious. She experienced painful menstruation, with nausea and severe cramps, forcing her to stay in bed the first day. The shock of the previous day had caused symptoms likened to a concussion. Convinced her life had taken a nasty turn, the young student was bewildered.

Secretly the mother applauded the move which would take her daughter away from the dangers of Main Street. This morning she looked at her, dying to hold her tight, entreating her to believe her: "Martha, I'd like to keep you here with me. I'm sorry to let you go into a world that despises my own. Later on, will you be willing to acknowledge me, the wife of an Indian, next to you, the wife of a White man? This world will tear us apart! I can feel it now, at a time when you are living your last hours in an environment I wish I could also leave behind. My dear girl, I have no choice. I have to risk it."

She added with greater assurance:
"Lady Luck is opening a door for you, Martha. Take this opportunity... You must."

Martha was hesitant about leaving her mother in this "dump." Common sense dictated she should stay with her parents.

"You're not Indian, Martha."

"But Mummy, I'm Métis."

"All the more reason to get closer to White people so no one will know."

"What about you? What will become of you?"

"Don't worry about me. I'm resigned to my fate."

"I'd like to be free of the shame of being Métis; I wish I could be proud of it."

"It's no use, Martha. Your parents can't help you. You'll have to depend on charity from the nuns to finish school. Believe me, if you want to escape poverty, hide your Métis 'nationality.' If you stay away from the Métis, you'll be lucky, because you don't speak with a Métis accent. You could always say you're an orphan."

"Why? I don't understand."

"If your father is in the picture, people will stay away from you. Have you noticed how much more "Indian" he looks as he gets older?"

"Yes, his Indian features are more obvious, but his physical appearance doesn't take away from his qualities. The girls in Lorette noticed Daddy when you came to the Christmas concert... I thought he was much better-looking than some of the slovenly Whites. He was clean and well-mannered. Have you ever considered living away from him?"

"Yes. Many times, especially when we lost our jobs at the Indian Residence. I knew poverty was just around the corner, and I just couldn't accept it. Your father is a big kid, but he's kind and wants to make me happy. After sixteen years of marriage, he still calls me "his White princess." I wanted to take you with me to Québec but it would have hurt him so much. Just the same I am convinced you wouldn't have any problems if we left Manitoba. In Québec, no one would guess you're Métis. You'll get a good job because you're bilingual."

"Mother! This is all so sad!"

"I stayed with your father because of Father Letendre. The morning of our marriage, he made me promise I would stand by your father all his life."

"And you kept your word for sixteen years? Poor Mummy. You're still a foreigner in this province where you have to speak English."

"In Manitoba, the French never really accept you. You need only three years to become an American citizen, but in Manitoba, after twenty-five years, you're still considered Québécois, or French, or American. It's not easy to understand... and impossible to explain. The Francophone minority needs the strength of numbers. At the beginning of this century a French colonist compared the Manitoba situation with France where a family is accepted only after four generations. But this will never be a problem for you: you're born in Manitoba, the only criteria the local Francophones consider valid. I think it's unfair. Those who have chosen to be Manitobans should command greater respect than those who were born here."

"I never imagined it would be so difficult to be accepted. Do you have an explanation for this?"

"I've never understood it. Sister Bernadette thinks Manitobans are tired of being told what to do by 'foreigners.' I think it's time I told you my secret. The day of your christening, I made a solemn promise you would live in a world other than my own. You're White, Martha, and you don't belong here."

"Couldn't we try to get ourselves out of this? We could move to Saint-Boniface. We'd at least be among French Canadians there."

"If the gentleman comes back to hire you, it'll be a good start. I'm waiting to hear from Sister Bernadette. She promised to find me a job... she's never let me down."

Robert arrived at the Star's around six o'clock in the afternoon. Fuelled by nervous energy, the two women did the dishes with lightning speed, and the mother had gone down to buy flowers from the poor Slavic woman in front of the corner grocery. Everyone knew she walked several miles each night, "visiting" the gardens of the well-to-do. The next day, she held between arthritic fingers the fruit of her night's labour. The custormer was rewarded with a yellow-toothed smile, and a tearful look of gratitude.

Gisèle had washed Martha's long black hair with fragrant shampoo and had done it up with two pink flowers. Dressed in a filmy white dress, the picture of freshness, Martha appeared as if out of a dream.

The teenager was far too pretty to live in this slum. No, Martha didn't belong in this neighbourhood; she had to be White or someone had transformed her.

The mother signalled to Martha to open the door.

"Yes. Well, you can't really be Martha Star?"

"Yes. I'm Martha."

"Come quickly. My mother is waiting for you downstairs," ordered Robert nervously.

That very evening, Martha moved in a large room in the Lavallées' home on Saint-Jean-Baptiste Street. The events of the day had upset her somewhat, so she slept little. How could she relax when she knew her mother was suffocating in the room she shared with her father? They had to close the window to get any sleep at all; the traffic never let up on the main road, and all the while, the neighbours, next door and upstairs, caroused all night.

Around two or three in the morning, when the revellers fell silent, they could open up a little to catch a bit of sleep; only too often, however, other noises started up, depriving everyone of deserved hours of sleep. Police sirens or fire trucks tore past, providing dramatic effect for the many misfortunes of this wretched area.

That summer, the Stars went to spend some time in the Fort Alexander Reserve: two weeks in July and two in August. Father Letendre had passed away. His successor, Father Chèvrefils, had witnessed the events surrounding Norman's trial. Sisters Beatrice, Thérèse and Simonne were still on staff.

The Oblate Fathers offered Norman a job, but Gisèle refused to live on an Indian reserve. Everyone was astonished. How could anyone choose Main Street over fresh air and unspoiled nature? For Gisèle, the reserve meant burying herself alive in a world she was beginning to reject. No, she would find her own way; she was determined to find a job in the city of Winnipeg, not in the fort Alexander Reserve or the village of Pine Falls. Gisèle was unshakable against the arguments of kind Father Chèvrefils; she pretended not to hear the list of all the temptations Norman would succumb to in Winnipeg. Taken aback by her show of stubbornness, the priest appealed to her reputed *profound* generosity. Finally, one more time, out of concern for Norman, and in the hope her unselfish attitude would be rewarded by Martha's success in the White man's world, Gisèle gave in and agreed to live in Fort Alexander. Her sacrifice was for Norman and Martha. Her own hopes and plans were cast aside once more... all for Norman and Martha!

Two reserve employees moved their pitiful furniture to new lodgings not far from their former residence. "What is Martha going to say?" Gisèle wondered, her face devoid of the sweetness of which the Indian women were so fond.

Near the shores of the Winnipeg River, the humble dwelling provided some comfort; the three freshly painted rooms were quiet and airy. Gisèle recognized the song of birds she had studied in school books: a thrush, a blue jay, an American robin. One day, she spotted a kingfisher swooping low, skimming the surface of the lake, and diving in; he flew away carrying a fish wriggling between its claws. She built two birdhouses to attract swallows and listen to their chattering.

Every morning, she experienced new life: the light of a new day, the sun warming the earth, gulls squealing, leaves rustling, prairie chickens clucking, waves lapping the shore. When all this started to bore her, she asked for a job at the Hudson's Bay Store. As for Norman, he had shed his depressed look since he was elected chief of Fort Alexander. He seemed happy, but Gisèle counted the number of times she left the gates of the reserve in late afternoon; before retiring, she put a mark on the calendar. The wings she felt in the morning, when she pushed the glass door of the store, turned to lead in the afternoon, when she removed her apron at the end of her day behind the pastry counter.

Norman dreamed of buying a car.

"You can't be serious," cried Gisèle.

"I'm the chief and several Indians have one."

"But you don't need one. You work on the reserve."

"We could go for rides on Sundays."

"Where to?"asked Gisèle. He hung his head.

The young woman guessed he had planned to ask for her savings. A loan! It was as well to make it a gift... the money she had saved, cent by cent, to pay Martha's tuition. Sister Superior at Lorette had advised her to be very careful.

"I'm not asking you anything," she said to Gisèle, "but promise me you'll save everything you earn."

Why had she been careless with her bank book? Now Norman knew there was money and coveted it. The subject of the car came up again and again; he had seen one, they had offered it cheap, he could even buy it on credit. A real bargain! Gisèle knew full well he would buy the car sooner or later, and stopped trying to oppose the purchase.

Living in the reserve with no other goal but to earn a few dollars, Gisèle felt the weight of the routine; her only wish was to survive another day. Occasionally, Father Chèvrefils kindly invited Gisèle to his office to telephone Martha.

Gisèle was pleased to hear Robert Lavallée was pursuing his studies in Ottawa. After his departure, Madame Lavallée had doubled, even tripled her physical exercises. With Martha's help she could use muscle-strengthening aids. She realized her thighs required more work than her legs, so she had asked for a therapist to come to her house two afternoons a week.

It was obvious Martha's dedication was responsible for the progress; she followed the doctor's orders religiously. One day, she noticed a job ad in the bank and inquired about it. The cashier told her about savings accounts and reasonable salary.

That same evening, Madame Lavallée noticed Martha was rather slow preparing dinner and eating less than usual. She inquired about her outing and her purchases. When she learned of Martha's plans to get an outside job, Madame Lavallée exclaimed:

"Martha, I can't manage without you! You're a fabulous girl. As neat as a nurse and sweet as an angel! I know it was hard for you to leave school, but don't give up on me, just when I'm hoping to walk some day. Look, I can move my upper legs from side to side; I can stretch out my legs without using my hands. Aren't you proud of me?" she added, smiling through her tears.

"Okay," said Martha, jumping up. She didn't want to see her patient overcome with tears. "Let's try for the thousandth time."

The young Métis girl grabbed Madame Lavallée by the waist so suddenly, her paralyzed legs slid off the sofa and onto the floor. Astounded, Madame Lavallée was standing in Martha's arms, but her legs were supporting her. The two women remained in one another's arms, afraid the least motion would cause the weak knees to buckle. The patient wanted to sit down, but her assistant protested.

"No, no... Try to remain standing for two minutes. Let's begin. I'll time you."

"Whew!" sighed Madame Lavallée, as she fell back into her armchair. "We have to call Robert tonight to tell him what I just did!"

"He won't believe you. Better call Jérôme."

"No. Robert first. At least he believes I can recover."

At the same time Madame Lavallée asked Robert his advice regarding Martha. Should she let her go?

At the other end, Robert was cheering. He kept repeating how anxious he was to see the miracle with his own eyes. He understood his mother's concern; but he sympathized with Martha. He felt she was too young to spend her life with an invalid, too bright to quit school, and too lively to give up all social activities, be it dancing or sports. He had played tennis with her a few times and she had strong arms and good legs. Lovely legs, too.

"Mom, I have an idea. A brain wave, really. Why don't you suggest she go back to school, but at St. Joseph's Academy? I know she left school reluctantly, and she'll probably agree to stay with you if she can go to the Academy as well."

Robert was right. Martha was delighted with the idea; she was grateful to Madame Lavallée for the change to her monotonous existence. It was already the end of October, but she would catch up with extra homework. Books, notebooks, pens, and math instruments piled up on her desk urging her to open her mind. She would use every spare moment and work overtime to get the best possible marks.

"You're working too hard," Madame Lavallée remarked from time to time.

"Okay then, let's invent new tricks to exercise your legs and give my brain a rest. Let's give those lazy thighs a good workout."

One morning, the patient announced proudly she had slipped out of bed during the night and had managed to get back without too much trouble.

"I am pleased for you, Madame Lavallée, but you haven't made as much progress since I went back to school. We wanted so much to surprise Robert when he comes for the Christmas vacation."

"You're right," the patient replied sadly. "I could spend more time in therapy, you know."

Martha looked at her for what seemed a long time, hesitated, then spoke:

"How about getting an assistant to replace me?"

"Not a chance! I feel so comfortable with you. I'm so appreciative; you're well-mannered, and so clean! You'd put the best maid to shame, to say nothing of the best nurse," the patient added teasingly.

"But it's for your own good!"

"Martha, have you thought of your mother?"

"My mother?"

"Yes. Would she like a job? She's only in her thirties. She could come for a few hours a day. Well, I don't even know if I can pay her. I have so little money."

"My mother would not expect anything in return for her work."

"That's not right. You should be earning more than your room and board for all the hours you spend with me. If we reduced your hours with me, you could study more, and have some free time. All that studying is fine, but you should be making friends and going out with other young people. Robert mentioned this on the phone."

Her son, usually such a tease, seemingly born to laugh; her son, living life to the hilt, her son had room to care and perhaps pity her a little. He had guessed she could, even at her age, have secret longings; she had been raised in a convent where, by the force of circumstances, you were cut off from love.

The following Friday, Martha made the long trip between Winnipeg and Pine Falls, a journey to her heritage, back to her Indian roots. Thinking of the identity she now suppressed, the experience revived strange feelings. Before she had had to make her way in the White man's world, she had been carefree and cheerful; in her teens she had been overwhelmed by a constant sadness; now, as she struggled to define her personality, she was no longer sure of the "real" Martha. At the Pine Falls bus station, all eyes turned towards the young White girl who followed the Indians to the old beaters in the parking lot. Martha asked an Indian if there was room for her.

"But we're going to the reserve. Do you want..."

"Yes, I'm going to my father's, Norman Star."

Martha was treated royally: they gave her the front seat, and wrapped her in a beautiful fur robe to protect her from the cold damp November evening. She pulled the robe up to her chin, recalling the famous exploits of the Métis in the buffalo hunt. She closed her eyes, imagining a pit covered with branches at the base of the cliff; when the animal fell in, it was hit with a volley of arrows. Martha heard the hooves of the wild horses introduced on the continent by the conquerors, superb horses from the South of the United States, and used to advantage by the settlers of the vast prairies.

The traveller was sorry the trip ended so soon: she was enjoying her flight of fantasy on the way to the reserve. The driver refused her dollar when he stopped in front of the Stars' home; he was honoured to have chauffeured the daughter of the chief's. He stood there, thanking her over and over, and shuffling his feet, just to go on admiring the lovely young lady from the city.

The mother greeted her daughter warmly, but the surprise visit left her speechless. Martha was devastated, as she held her mother close, realizing the extent of her distress. What could be the cause of such despair? She caressed her mother's gaunt face, trying to stop her tears. In her imagination, she saw her mother in the flower garden of the Winnipeg Indian residence; the picture of happier days enabled her to speak:

"Daddy?"

"He's in bed, very ill. Martha! If you only knew..

Six

"Mummy," pleaded Martha, "don't miss the chance of a lifetime. If you put Daddy in the hospital, you can come and live with me at Madame Lavallée's. You remember, when I was the one hesitating about leaving Main Street? You said: 'It's a chance of a lifetime. Now it's my turn to say it.'"

"I can't abandon your father just when he needs me most. He'll die of boredom in a hospital, I know him."

"What's his sickness, do we know?"

"Cancer. He'll be gone in a few months."

While Norman slept, mother and daughter talked late into the night; they were searching for a solution to satisfy all three. The Pine Falls Hospital was too far from Saint-Boniface for Gisèle to visit her husband every day; besides, if she kept her job, she could stay on the reserve.

Norman had bought the coveted automobile, but had been involved in an unfortunate accident. Once in hospital, he was made aware of the deterioration of his health; alarmed by the diagnosis, he swore to never again set foot in such a place.

The next day, Martha went to the Indian reserve. Alone in the chapel, after Sunday mass, she tried to make sense of events; the more she prayed, the more confused she became. How was she going to concentrate on her studies if her mother had to take care of her father? Her mother maintained she had to place her father in an institution. Just the same... when they had wanted to take Madame Lavallée out of her own home, Robert insisted they listen first of all to the person whose fate was being determined. Martha decided she would ask her father to voice his opinion regarding his own future. Absorbed in her prayers, her head in her hands, Martha heard a voice announcing Father Chèvrefils requested an interview in his office.

The Father Superior wanted to put her up to date on his conversation with Norman. He had only one wish: to return to his familiar corner in Winnipeg, near his friends. Hearing this, Martha wondered if her wish had already been answered. Not so for her mother. The change would make her life even more difficult. In Fort Alexander, she could at least leave the reserve six days a week. Furthermore, her job allowed her to see other Whites. "Poor Mummy," Martha whispered.

It took three days to find a home in Winnipeg, close the house in Fort Alexander, and move the family down. As they had done so many times in the past, the Oblate missionaries' generosity bordered on heroism. The Indians who came to bid Norman farewell expressed their regret at losing their young chief who had introduced many necessary reforms.

Although Gisèle did not voice her opinion, secretly she wished she had had the courage to oppose the sick man's decision, expecting people to consider her needs. She did not dare protest in front of Father Chèvrefils, and Martha, both concerned with Norman's welfare. However much she had been reluctant to return to the Indian reserve, now their departure seemed totally wrong. She had to give up the beauty and fresh air of Lake Winnipeg, the clean house and the flower garden, her salary, the birds, and little squirrels she had tamed. On the eve of their departure, she went for a solitary walk on the shore of the bewitching lake, to scold the Machi-Manitou, the god responsible for evil and misery in this world.

Once her parents were settled in Winnipeg, Martha saw them more frequently. She went in quietly, opened the window and sat at the sick man's bedside. The noise of traffic at the corner of Main and Sutherland was enough to drive one mad; it drowned out any attempt at conversation. He stared at his daughter. Did he recognize her? Suddenly, he looked down, apparently ashamed of the thoughts invading his consciousness.

"Martha... I wish I could have..."

"It's okay, Daddy. Don't you fret. We love you, Mummy and I. You did your best, but Indians who have any luck in life are few and far between."

Gisèle tiptoed into the room. "Norman, do you remember the residence on Academy Road where Martha was born?"

"I wish your mother... could have been a real princess."

"You're dreaming again, Norman," continued Gisèle. She was dreaming, too. "First, you must get well and we'll start again. Martha is lucky. She's keeping up with her studies and doing well. As for us, we..."

"I'm going to die. I know it. The doctor told me. It's you I'm sad about. You're sorry you had anything do with me, aren't you?"

There was a knock at the door, and Gisèle left the room. Norman wouldn't see her tears. Martha, trying to compose herself, got up and poured her father a glass of juice. While he drank, she looked carefully at his face. He was thirty-eight years old, and looked fifty. His hair was still jet black, but he was missing two lower teeth and had a scar across his forehead. Where had he suffered a beating, in Winnipeg or Pine Falls? Indians who happened to be in the wrong place were often treated with brutality. Martha was about to ask him, when her mother came in:

"Two friends of yours, Norman. Do you want to get up?"

Luke Jones and Paul Courchesne had come to visit: they were both guitarists, formerly players in the Fort Alexander band. Martha was taken aback by the pitiful appearance of the two visitors; she got up to leave. In any case, they would not have uttered a single word in the presence of the two women: they had always felt intimidated by their friend's White wife and now his daughter...

Gisèle and Martha went downstairs and took Austin Street to get away from the Main Street racket. The houses along the sidewalk were disfigured by obscene graffiti, as if taunting the magnificent nearby church. Towards the western side, a bold sun beamed its pure warm rays onto passersby.

The two women sat on the steps of the cathedral below the superb stained glass windows, admired by all connoisseurs. Mother and daughter took advantage of a few minutes of privacy. It was Martha's opportunity to get straight to the point:

"Your apartment is a disaster, Mummy. The smell permeates the walls. It turns my stomach. I just can't get used to it. Every time I come..."

"I knew what to expect... I wanted to stay over there..."

"I'm sorry,"Martha interjected. "I feel guilty now. I should have thought of you as much as of Daddy. You were right. Your house in Fort Alexander was a palace compared to this."

Gisèle had tried to clean up the apartment. The downstairs grocer had given her some paint in return for occasional help behind the counter. It had killed the smell of mildew in the bedroom now too dark under its coat of blue paint. As for the bathroom, it would take more than paint to destroy the odour of urine and excrement. Once a week, Gisèle scrubbed the viscous wooden floor; one day, she even contemplated pouring a bottle of benzene down the toilet; afterwards, she could "accidentally" drop a lighted match, "just to purify the air," she thought. It was no solution: it would simply mean more humiliating negotiations to seek refuge in yet another cheap "dump."

Martha was astounded to hear her mother curse and swear through her tears. Nevertheless she understood the profound reason for this outburst, and rocked her mother in her arms, while fishing out a supply of tissues from her handbag.

On this November afternoon, the air was intoxicating; the large elms shivered in the sunshine, their last leaves a soft covering on the paved driveway leading to the steps of the church. The crunchy golden carpet seemed so inviting, a playground for the silly squirrel glancing here and there, waving its elegant tail. Gisèle was despondent... so tired of living, of hoping for better days.

The wind brushed patterns on the faces and hands of the two dejected creatures; from time to time, passersby paused, forcing a smile, then hurried on their way. Was Gisèle destined to a life of poverty and despair? She considered returning to Québec. Was that a solution? She would have liked to voice her doubts. But then... there was Martha: she was finding her way. Was it fair to snatch her away from the environment where she was thriving? Could she leave her alone in Manitoba? Either alternative was heart-wrenching.

"Mummy, are you really going to spend the next six months watching Daddy die?"

"What else can I do?"

"If he was in an institution, you could visit him every day. The social worker who placed me with the Lavallées..."

"Martha, since you left Main Street, I haven't wished for anything more."

Martha knew Gisèle was lying.

"You're wrong. You're only thirty-four and in good health. When you curl your hair, you're so pretty. You could find a job... go out each day... see people... make friends..."

Wearing Madame Lavallée's hand-me-down skirt and sweater, Gisèle certainly did not look her age; many a well-to-do Winnipegger would have envied her physical attributes. The red wool sweater put a blush on her satiny complexion; the straight skirt revealed a girlish figure.

She blushed at the compliment and recalled an incident from her past: one day an elder from Fort Alexander had teased Norman: "Aha! you marry White woman and have White daughter." Their happiness at being together then was overshadowed by their isolation at social events. Once, at a friend's wedding in Lorette, Gisèle was hurt when she realized everyone was simply ignoring her husband. He hadn't dared ask anyone else to dance, although he was by far the best dancer in the hall. The pair had spent the evening dancing cheek to cheek, very much aware of their special "status" at the gathering.

"Mummy, you're a million miles away!"

"I was dreaming of what I've become. Neither White nor Indian. I just hope you'll be able to manage."

"I'll get by, you'll see. I'm Métis. It's an advantage."

"Not necessarily."

"Do you mean I'll always feel different, the way I do at the Academy?"

"You could be treated as a second-class citizen, compared to the girls from "good families" as they say. The Métis are classless people. It is a pity, but everyone forgets the contribution these people made to the development of Manitoba. You should have heard Sister Bernadette talking about the voyageurs who worked for the fur trading companies and who married Indian women. Without the help of the Métis many settlers would have never survived the beginnings of the colony."

The two women were near the lamp post, when a tramp came towards them.

"He's begging," whispered Gisèle timidly.

"No, I don't want any money. I'm not a beggar. I heard you speaking in French. It's not often we hear French in these parts. It's mostly Indians here."

He went on, picking up on their conversation; White men should marry White women, and Indians take Indian wives. He had himself been a victim of the racial differences; his wife had run away with a White man, leaving him with three children; later she came back with two more kids. Since then, his life was a mess.

The two women listened to his diatribe, but remained powerless to give the poor man a glimmer of hope; they found no comforting words to temper his sadness. They went down the steps of the portico and stood on either side of the unfortunate wretch. The stranger's revelations had put an end to their moaning: at least the three Stars had always been together.

They wished their new friend the best of luck, and quickly walked up towards Main Street, before darkness fell in the lanes and corners fraught with danger. Here and there, girls had taken their positions, awaiting a generous hand or the warmth of another body in a temporary lodging. The scene reminded Gisèle of another occasion; her first love-making in the Aberdeen Hotel. She shivered, grabbed Martha's arm, and hurried them on their way.

Inside the Stars' apartment, the light was on in the empty kitchen. The bedroom was deserted... Norman was gone!

Seven

One Saturday morning in December, Martha arrived at her mother's with the intention of forcing her to go out; her excuse was she absolutely needed a quiet place to finish an essay on *Hamlet*.

"Of course," Gisèle said, holding back her tears, "a little break from this prison will do me a world of good... It's depressing to spend your life between these four walls; it's not healthy to be alone so much with morbid thoughts."

The woman was apparently in a nervous state: she cried over every little thing; her loss of control was affecting her morale. Her apartment, stifling in summer, was ice-cold in winter; bundled up in two sweaters and wool socks, she seemed to have aged ten years. Martha was pleasantly surprised her offer was accepted so spontaneously; perhaps her mother had had enough of her isolation. Thank heaven for that! She hoped to save her from a nervous breakdown.

"Take the time to do what you want today!" Martha advised. "You can spend some time at Eaton's and then go and see Madame Lavallée. Here, take this money. Sister Superior gave it to me for doing junior study hall supervision."

Martha sat by the kitchen window. She found it difficult to concentrate on her class notes; the poor lighting annoyed her, and she could feel her father's presence in the apartment. She pictured him at the table, or standing at the window, his hands on his hips, bent forward trying to catch a glimpse of clean sky.

Two months and still no news of him. Two months while her mother insisted on waiting for the runaway. This time, she guessed what Madame Lavallée and her mother would talk about; she would at least win this round.

But she was in for a surprise. Robert appeared at the door around half past twelve. He had returned two days sooner, having exchanged his ticket with a friend forced to stay behind to redo an assignment for a finicky professor. Martha would have preferred not to see Robert again in her parents' apartment. In a letter she had implied this one was cleaner than the first. Now she truly regretted hiding the truth. But who could have thought Robert would ever come here again?

She was filled with shame: the worn-out furniture, the torn linoleum, the curtains all askew, the sink surrounded by grey metal sheeting, the frayed rug under Robert's feet; he was so handsome in his light blue windbreaker, his scarf slung jauntily around his neck. Her bright eyes were drawn to his unruly hair. But he caught her glance and, with one swoop of his long slender fingers, he swiftly rearranged the rebellious locks. He laughed heartily, tossing his head back, and dropping his one hundred and fifty pounds in the creaky old rocking chair.

Robert was oblivious to the ugliness of the dwelling; he was staring at Martha, and talking a blue streak. Martha relaxed, reassured by the attitude of a visitor who had the gift of making poor people feel important, treating them with respect and consideration.

Seeing the little margarine container and bowl of soup on the rickety table, Robert suggested:

"My mother sent me to get you. But let's leave the two ladies to their chatting."

"How did you find my mother?"

"A little discouraged, but my own mother will cheer her up, don't worry. No news from your father?"

"Not a thing."

"Listen, Martha, let me take you to a restaurant. I'm starved. And we can have a visit."

In the car, Martha finally expressed her feelings:

"I'm so happy to see you. When you think, I'm studying a 17th-century tragedy while my parents are living this drama; it's pretty weird. I think I should be trying to solve my family problems."

"It's true, your father deserted; but you should know Indians hate institutions where their freedom is limited. The idea of going to hospital must have frightened him. I'll bet he's living on a reserve somewhere, with his two friends."

"My father's not a real Indian."

"I agree he lived like a White man for a number of years; but don't you think this flight is an attempt to return to his roots?"

"I'd like to find him if only to relieve my mother's distress."

"You'll have problems discovering his hiding place. Indians know how to keep a secret. If I were you, I'd try to come to terms with the situation, and stop waiting for him. Anyway, choose a restaurant." Robert wanted to change the subject. This conversation was too depressing on such a bright winter's day.

"You choose. It doesn't matter." She almost added: "as long as I'm with you."

"Whew!" sighed Robert with a laugh."I was afraid you'd choose the Beefeater. Let's go to Warren's Corner. To afford this trip I had to cut corners, and it's going to be tight paying for my trip back."

Leading the way into the restaurant, Martha felt proud to be in the company of such a fine-looking guy. Robert managed to steer the meal-time conversation away from her problems. What a relief to hear her youthful laughter and to see her so relaxed.

Robert kept to himself the conversation he had had with an Oblate father who knew hundreds of Indians, and who had assured him Norman Star's case was nothing to worry about. Having determined to act on this "mission impossible," he now doubted the desirability of his intervention. After all, Norman Star was happy wherever he was. He avoided any mention of the runaway.

"Martha, my mother has progressed twice as fast as the therapist had predicted. Now, I'd like to return the favour by helping your mother."

"Well, your mother might be walking now if I hadn't returned to school. I feel guilty about not spending as much time with her."

"Don't be sorry. You were right to think of yourself," he said, placing his slender white hand on Martha's short stubby fingers. "For the moment, your mother could come and stay with us. I can sleep in the den in the basement: that's the purpose of our mothers' conversation this afternoon. You saw the orderly mess in the basement?» Robert asked with a chuckle. "If your mother accepts, I'll tidy up my books in no time. I'd even stay in the garage to get your mother away from Main Street."Martha felt her pulse quickening.

She wanted to give Robert a big hug. First, he had saved her; now her mother. She looked at him closely, trying to guess the motives for his generosity; he seemed so gentle, so warm... He was just a dream!

She enjoyed the weight of his arm around her shoulders as he opened the door for her; in the car, puzzled by his prolonged gaze, her heart beat faster. What did this mean? She felt confused, the same as when he had appeared at her door: her heart skipped a beat, her stomach knotted as if she had had too much to eat. She took a deep breath; she wouldn't let herself get carried away. She had to think.

To love someone without being loved in return? No way. Robert would never guess her feelings when he touched her. Her own parents' marriage had been disastrous, and she had learned her lesson. Her Métis blood burned ardently in her veins... She would feign indifference even though she felt like throwing her arms around him. She imagined herself nestled in his arms, his lips burning on hers in a passionate embrace. But she had no time to affirm her resolve. Robert cried:

"Let's play a trick on your mother. Let's get her things and keep her with us tonight. What do you think?"

Martha dissolved. She sought refuge in his arms. He was only too pleased to cover her sensual mouth with a burning kiss.

"Thank you, Robert."

"You're great, Martha."

Eight

Robert had hoped his college friend would come to Saint-Boniface for the Christmas break; but Doris Gardner was so proud and unpredictable he hadn't dared mention it to anyone. Anyway, he wasn't really expecting her.

With Gisèle helping Lucille Lavallée, the two young people were free to go out and have fun. With a difficult first semester behind him, Robert was restless; and Martha needed some fresh air before the Christmas exams. Magnificent Bird's Hill Park became their daily refuge. Every afternoon, when Martha came out of St. Joseph's Academy, there was Robert, beeping the horn of the old Dodge; he had packed snowshoes, scarves and mittens in the trunk. On the back seat—a camera to capture the splendid views at sunset.

With incredible energy, they trudged through sparkling bluish stillness. Martha had to be hard on herself, just as in real life: keep going forward, you're not there yet; set your goals, aim for your dreams. So you want to be more than ordinary? Right on! She recalled the text of her eighth grade English textbook: "Make the most of your stuff." She had taken the phrase as her motto, set it to music, and hummed it to herself. On many occasions she had heard an old Irish nun say "Hold your head high." Smiling at the vast skies above, Martha was compelled to try even harder to catch up with Robert.

Her life would be just like today: committed and enthusiastic, she would take huge steps and leave footprints as deep as those she left behind her now. And why couldn't her life be exhilarating? The traces she left in the snow confirmed her efforts and determination; Robert, in the lead, seemed to be skating along. He slowed down if she asked him, or paused to admire the tiny woman struggling with the cumbersome snowshoes.

Later, they planned to go to a chalet at the north end of the park; Robert would order two enormous hamburgers, fried onion rings, and root beer. Near the crackling fire, they could remove their parkas and tuques, blow warm breath on numb fingers, then rub noses and cheeks back to life. In the restaurant, men and women, and famished children boasted of their prowess, while Robert, alone with Martha in a much-longed-for tête-à-tête, gazed at her lovingly.

Escaping to nature became the highlight of Robert and Martha's student life, their reason for existence. They left behind essays to be written, boring lectures and compulsory reading. They delighted in the sparkling beauty of their surroundings, ears filled with the song of the wind enveloping them, nostrils sniffing the bracing prairie air, inflating their hungry chests.

Without Robert, Martha would never have explored the remote corners of the provincial park, nor enjoyed its virgin wilderness; Robert could stage a premeditated fall, as a pretext to rock Martha in his arms. Oh, how she loved the pretence! And how he wrapped himself around her, covering her completely....He could tame his athletic body to total stillness. The Bird's Hill sun smiled knowingly, content to shine on this little island of happiness. Only they knew the source of the blue stain left by Robert's clothing on the white surface; the sighs and sweet words of love were for their ears alone.

That afternoon at the restaurant, Martha was dying to dance, wrapped in Robert's arms. She clung to him, hungering for his touch. Poor girl! How could she have guessed at that very moment, he was choosing his words to prepare her for Doris' visit? He couldn't bring himself to make the announcement, hoping to enjoy as long as possible the company of the girl he had compared to "the English girl from Ottawa." The "bad news"was secure in the pocket of his jacket. What a mess! If only he had waited to tell Martha of his love!

Doris expected him to be "proper," as did her mother he had met once at the National Arts Centre in Ottawa; she reminded him of the Queen of England, with her manners, poise, language, and her little old-fashioned pillbox hat. He couldn't help thinking: "Doris is going to be as starchy as she is." "Good Heavens! What am I doing on board this galley ship?"

The Lavallée household was much more cheerful with Robert home for the holidays and Gisèle helping out. One Saturday, Martha was up early to finish some school work due before the Christmas break. Later she planned to have a talk with her mother about her dates with Robert and her feelings towards him. It was well overdue. On several occasions, her mother had put forth leading questions, but each time she pretended not to catch on.

"You're playing with fire," Gisèle remarked gently, after hearing Martha's account of their last outing. "Robert knows your background; you had better forget about him before..."

Martha buried her head against her mother's shoulder, before her eyes betrayed the depth of her involvement. Unable to determine whether the hurt was due to love or her incapability of giving up, she sobbed her heart out, her face pressed to her mother's warm cheek.

"He knows you're Métis. He has only one thing in mind... you know what it is..."

Martha was turning out to be a beauty: short wavy hair showed off to good advantage a face and throat resplendent with youthful freshness. Her slightly oriental eyes and round figure gave her a childlike appearance, typical of the Métis people. Many White people could never figure out the racial origins of the Métis and often asked: "Italian or Spanish?"Martha had been asked that question many times.

Now that her mother had made her views known, Martha determined to follow her intuition, but to be on her guard. Nevertheless, she gave in, and, on the last Friday in December, invited Robert to the dance at the St. Boniface Youth Centre.

Her red silk dress accentuated her figure, high heels showing off her legs, and adding a little height to her almost-five feet. As they were getting ready to leave, Madame Lavallée invited Martha to choose a piece of jewelry from her case: instinctively, the young man picked out a pearl necklace and bracelet for her.

The evening would have been perfect if it hadn't been for the many bold intrusions: every time a friend cut in to dance with Martha, Robert felt miserable, seeing her with a rival. He watched his chance to take her away again, holding her close. Martha was really letting loose, but not totally deaf to her mother's warning still ringing in her ears.

"Martha, please dance only with me tonight," Robert whispered. Resolution overshadowed the disappointment in his voice.

Snuggled as she was against the handsome figure, Martha would have promised a lifetime of dances. When he insisted, she muttered:

"Why?"

"Can't you guess?" he asked, his lips wandering to the edge of her low-cut dress.

Martha felt herself weakening; once again, she forgot her mother's warning and buried her tearful eyes against his shoulder. She sighed:

"Whatever will be, will be."

"What did you say?"

"I don't know," Martha replied.

Surprised, Robert held her still closer; wrapped in his arms, she hoped to drink in words of love such as he had spoken this last week, but none were forthcoming. Martha believed she was the cause of his eloquent silence. Why didn't he tell her he loved her, as he had so often during their snowshoe outings?

Serious and thoughtful, Robert held her in his arms, his face buried in her soft hair. Once again, he was sorry he had spoken.

Martha had never heard of Doris Gardner from either Robert or Madame Lavallée; her impromptu arrival on December 28th, therefore, was cause for some confusion. The visitor's clothes said a lot regarding the financial situation of her Toronto parents. So, when Martha sat beside her at table, opposite Robert, she pictured the contrast. Having convinced herself she didn't stand a chance in this wicked contest, Martha rebelled inwardly. She imagined a double-cross, and her heart sank.

In the company of four women, three of whom were almost totally silent, Robert wasn't having much success at orchestrating relaxed conversation. He was rightfully embarrassed, but would have felt even worse had he been able to gauge the true measure of their displeasure. Throwing a rival into the game, at a time when his mother was delighted he was spending time with Martha to distract her from her studies, was an unforgivable faux-pas. Lucille Lavallée approved of Robert's rare outings, and tried to convince Gisèle Star to allow the innocent relationship between the two students. However, Doris' arrival had upset her just as Gisèle Star was suffering from Martha's humiliation.

In the course of the conversation Doris Gardner repeatedly boasted about her family. Her father was a lawyer of considerable reputation, her mother a gynecologist at the Ottawa General Hospital; one brother was an engineer, and another was studying dental surgery. Gisèle and Martha feigned genuine interest, so the girl would keep on talking, thus avoiding being themselves the subject of the customary questions.

What could they say, to the usual «What does your father do? And your husband?» Occupation being everything to snobs and the well-heeled, down-to-earth Gisèle had little to offer: housewife with a runaway Indian husband...

When the one responsible for this ludicrous situation guessed Gisèle and her daughter were uncomfortable, he changed the subject to politics, theatre and travel. It was a lost cause! Doris managed to find a point to brag about someone in her family, so she again commanded all the attention.

Her Wonder-Bra bust in a superb boutique sweater, Doris was well aware of her glamour-girl image. As the meal progressed, Martha raged. Seething in anger, she thought she would explode, grab the long blonde mane, and shake sense into the silly head; she saw red, mad at Robert Lavallée and wishing she could throw something at him, a chicken leg dripping with gravy, maybe.

After the cheese and strawberry mousse, when Madame Lavallée suggested they have coffee in the living room, Martha excused herself to help her mother in the kitchen. Robert followed Doris to the piano where she played his favourite song: the one-man audience was constantly turning towards the door, anxiously awaiting Martha's return. The air was heavy. Three women to do the dishes... Robert knew he had hurt Martha, and would have gladly scoured a hundred pots. The silly show he was putting on for the unwanted visitor made him feel more than ridiculous.

Some time later, when Gisèle and Lucille came back to the living room, Robert was unable to hide his disappointment.

"Where's Martha? Still in the kitchen?"

"No, she went up to her room," Madame Lavallée admitted.

He grabbed the banister, climbed the steps two at a time, and went down the hallway to Martha's room:

"Martha, it's me. Open up, I want to explain. Martha, please open the door. Let me in, please. There's nothing between Doris and me. Doris is just a classmate from University; she wanted to come to Winnipeg. I couldn't refuse. Listen to me..."

Nine

Snowflakes mix with her tears as she walks along Hamel Avenue, her white-mittened hands holding her fur collar up around her head. The calm evening air quells her rage. Wishing to pace her escape, she lengthens her stride, and bows her head; the crescent moon is showing a pleasant face, in contrast to the girl's state of mind.

There is someone behind her. The steps come closer, faster. She is being followed. Robert? Someone running to catch the bus on *Des Meurons* Street? The person is close on her heels; she steps off the sidewalk to let him pass. She turns quickly only to face a man opening his coat to expose his naked body.

The aimless walker lets out such a scream as to make the maniac turn around and disappear as mysteriously as he had come. Blinded by fear, Martha trips and falls in the middle of the street. Her cries echo in the silence of the night, not a door opens, not a single porch light comes on. She struggles to her feet, and thinks of Sister Suzanne.

Ten minutes later, Martha was safe in the familiar music studio. She snuggled into a cozy leather chair. Telling her story had a soothing effect on her panic-stricken state: her encounter with the flasher, her feelings, Robert, the much-too-attractive visitor.

"I'm jealous, Sister, and I'm ashamed. I fled like a wild creature, admitting my weakness."

"You're overreacting, Martha," replied the sister convincingly.

The convent girls agreed Sister Suzanne could write many a novel—on the romantic adventures of her music students. One does not teach for twenty years in a girls' school without becoming attuned to their lives outside the institution... unless one is deaf, blind and insensitive.

As far as Sister Suzanne was concerned, Martha's present crisis was a normal stage. A fit of jealousy merely confirmed her attachment to Robert.

"You know what you have to do to put an end to your feeling of shame? Show them you can be independent; hold your head high. Don't let Miss Gardner or Robert know your feelings. You're every bit as good as they are. So prove it."

"But I've been humiliated," Martha mumbled. "I should have thought it over before running away like this."

"You don't have to account to anyone about where you go. Just say you had an appointment and you forgot to take leave. A major breach of etiquette!" the sister added, jokingly.

"What about tomorrow morning?"

"Tomorrow, get up and go do your shopping."

"Shopping! With what money?"

"I have a hundred dollars I want to give you, Martha. You heard right. A hundred dollars! Buy yourself a skirt, or a new sweater, or even a dress... Just browsing through the stores will take your mind off things. I can get the convent car and take you if you wish; afterwards, we'll celebrate your escape in a little restaurant. Don't tell the Lavallées where you're going."

"Have you robbed the alms box? We've been trying so hard to get donations since September."

"I'm going to tell you a secret. It's a real secret, you understand? At the secondary school, there was a sister—she's dead now—who used to give my brother money because our family was so poor. Bernard never forgot her kindness. Later when he started to earn a salary, he sent her money regularly so she could continue to help young people as she saw fit. As time went on, he earned a better salary, and gave even more, so in turn she could help more poor people who tried to hide their need. He loved this sister who knew how to give without making people feel put down. She might pay way too much for some job or other, but the boys guessed she was well-intentioned: she only wanted to help the less fortunate without hurting their feelings. Now it's my turn to be my brother's ambassador. It's not an easy role to play... the giver always feeling generous, her conscience at peace.

The hundred dollars I'm offering you today come from my brother. You supervised the music students several times since October, and I haven't paid you. You've earned that money. So, will you take it?"

The next morning, Robert was taken aback when he saw a rather exuberant Martha. Around two in the afternoon, a girl rang the doorbell to invite her to a hockey game between the Saints and the Mohawks. Robert pulled back the curtains discreetly. There were two boys in the car. Well! He watched Jeanne Martel and Martha going down the path, arm in arm, laughing and giggling.

"Sister Suzanne is the best match-maker!" he heard Jeanne exclaim.

On New Year's Eve, Martha left the house without telling anyone at the Lavallées' about her trip. Robert inquired, but Gisèle did not reveal the content of the note she had found pinned to the pillow case. He wanted to show off in front of his rich classmate... "let him pay for his foolishness," Gisèle decided.

Doris Gardner slept late, and Robert did the rounds on the neighbouring streets: Taché, de la Cathédrale, Provencher and Aulneau. Surely, Martha hadn't left town, she must be at a friend's.

Jeanne Martel was surprised to see Robert at her door. No, Martha was not here. Yes, they had been out together the day before, with the two Gendron boys. No, she hadn't said if she was planning anything. Touched by his concern, Jeanne promised to call several classmates.

Robert spent a miserable day feeling guilty about the embarrassing situation he had caused at home, and the flight of a girl who was more than just a good friend. Doris was gloating. She was well aware of the attention Robert paid to his mother's protégée.

"You're stuck on the little Half-Breed girl, aren't you? You're so upset, you've lost your appetite," Doris said sarcastically, as they went down the front steps. "You hardly touched your steak... knowing how much you like meat..."

"Her mother is worried."

"Not as much as you are," Doris added mockingly.

Robert was hurt. He closed the car door on her with such force, she knew she had gone too far. Hell! What had made him invite the girl to Winnipeg? He had spoken without thinking one night at Paul Dubois' when she had all the guys under her spell. To win a bet, he would try to conquer Doris Gardner.

In the evening, at a party at Brian Lecompte's, Doris was the centre of attention. Everyone agreed Robert knew how to land gorgeous girls. With all the guys vying for Doris' attention, Robert danced with Martha's friends, hoping they would tell him of her whereabouts. At the end of the evening, glancing over his partner's shoulder he saw Doris wrapped around Brian, like a circus snake. He hated her.

The next day, annoyed at his mother's silence, Robert blurted out:

"I just want to explain; she's been gone four days. If she knew the facts about Doris' visit to Saint-Boniface, she'd come back. I swear there's nothing between Doris and me; less than nothing, I can't wait for her to leave. Where is Martha, anyway?"

"Gisèle promised Martha she wouldn't give away her secret. Can't you see her mother is upset and confused over this affair? It's spoiled our Christmas... and she's angry at you for hurting her daughter."

"Mother, please." Robert spoke more calmly now. "In November when I invited Doris here, Martha was working as a servant in this house. And then, we started going out, skiing and snowshoeing, and talking, and after our date on the 28th of December, I saw her differently. Anyway, this morning I've decided to put off my trip back to Ottawa."

Lucille Lavallée smiled and placed a reassuring hand on her son's shoulder:

"You'll see her again. Trust me."

Robert was despondent, not as a thwarted lover, feeling he'd lost out on a good thing; rather he showed remorse at having hurt an amazingly sensitive and candid young woman. Martha would occupy his thoughts for days. Things were even worse when he got to Ottawa, because she had not reappeared before his departure.

In the plane he told Doris he wanted to sleep; rather than make an effort at conversation with a girl he was no longer interested in, he chose to replay his blunder over in his mind, thus hoping to be properly remorseful. If only he could transfer the hurt entirely to his own heart, he might take away Martha's pain. A romantic violin melody penetrated his every pore, soothing his tired nerves, filling him with a healing lethargy. Doris was reading the *Winnipeg Free Press.* Eyes closed, Robert recalled Martha's features: strange eyes in a pure clean face. He pictured the precious photos, hidden away in the right pocket of his coat. His favourite showed Martha in the middle of a stand of birches in Bird's Hill Park.

Grinning from ear to ear, she appeared out of the earth, like a little snow goddess, bringing good news, before the crocuses sprung out. The sun's bright rays converged on her, enveloping her with mystery in the immense white landscape. The million kisses—as they stood together, trying to be close in spite of the cumbersome snowshoes—had been the happiest moments of his life; he could feel, even now, Martha's cold cheeks and puckered lips on his face.

On January 8th, the phone rang while he was in the shower.

"Mother? What's going on? Can you speak up?"

"I'm in my bedroom. I don't want them to hear. Martha returned last night. She's behaving strangely. I don't know if I should talk about you."

"How is she different? Is she ill? Do talk to her about me; you'll see how she reacts."

"She's been so cold. She talks to me like a stranger. I'm afraid they're both going to leave me."

"I just wrote to her. Watch her reaction when you give her my letter."

"Okay. I'll do that. I'll wait for the letter."

"If I could afford it, I'd go to Winnipeg for the weekend. Easter break is just too far away."

Lucille didn't detect any reaction as she handed her the letter. The girl simply slipped it into her pocket. Was she being coy?

"Do you think you could give me a bath? Your mother has a lot of errands to do."

Martha, apparently guessing Lucille's intentions, seemed overly enthusiastic.

"Sure! For sure! No problem!"

Lucille Lavallée needed the hot soapy water, the slow friction of the coarse brush, to relax and revive her legs. Bathing and massaging, Martha chatted away, taking care not to venture onto treacherous ground, avoiding all show of emotion. For her part, Lucille wanted to reestablish their relationship.

Snug in her powder pink dressing gown, Lucille was on her feet, looking at herself in the mirror, as she waited for Martha to bring her wheelchair in from the hallway. Seeing Martha standing in the doorway, she was about to say something, when she heard an order:

"No chair today. You have two legs."

"What?"

"I said: you have two legs. Today's the day. Walk."

Lucille's mind raced: Robert, Jérôme, Martha, Gisèle. She concentrated all her efforts. A step for each one of them. Robert, her youngest; he phoned all the time, he reminded her of his support, his belief in her will power. For Robert, she raised her right foot; she overbalanced with the effort, but the foot went down correctly, in front. Lucille wavered, but caught her balance at once.

"Great!" cheered Martha, both arms in the air like a hockey fan. "If you can take one step, you can take two, why not three? Four? Put as much effort on your left foot, the lazy one. Go on. If you can't, I'm right here."

The left side! It was still so weak! If only she could show him, the son who thought she wouldn't get better, who advised her to sell the house. If she walked, she could take her grandson out near Provencher Park. Jérôme would come more often; he couldn't bear the sight of an invalid. Here goes! The left foot moved quicker than she expected and came down near the right.

No wavering, no faltering. Completely astounded, Lucille nevertheless remained erect and confident, her eyes full of excitement, glowing and triumphant. Three more steps and she would be safe in Martha's open arms. She gathered all her strength and overcame her fear with supreme dignity.

Martha was deeply touched by the sick woman's tears of joy. Stroking her frail shoulders, she gently reproached her patient:

"Come now. There's enough humidity in the bathroom. Stop the tears. No. Go ahead and cry. Scream if you want to, if it makes you feel better."

After her return form Kenora, Martha had tried to free herself from her nurse's role, but the unexpected success or her efforts touched her deeply. She let her emotions take over, a welcome relief for the pain she had endured. The tears flowed as she turned her sweet face towards the woman who was totally transformed with gratitude.

Lucille held on to Martha, thanking her out loud, silently praising God, and shedding tears of joy. At that moment, she was able to cast aside all the fears she had entertained those many months, when her progress was so slow, and she had come to suspect even Martha was doubting the possibility of recovery. The nightmare was over!

On the other hand, Martha felt renewed strength: she felt she would always be close to this courageous woman who happened to be Robert's mother. She had just witnessed a miracle. With determination and perseverance, she thought, you could always see your way out of difficult situations.

"I'm walking! Look! I'm walking!" cried Madame Lavallée.

"You're walking! I can see you. You're walking!" Martha echoed.

Joined in a shared ecstasy, which woman transmitted the thought to the other? No one would ever know. But they looked at each other, and cried in one voice:

"Robert!"

·

Ten

Martha had refused Sister Suzanne's money; she had also refused to see the very snobbish Claude Gendron who had asked her why she lived at the Lavallées'. In any case, Sister Suzanne, who had more than one string to her bow, never gave up on a student in need; therefore, she had invited Martha to their Kenora convent, on Lake of the Woods in Ontario. This would afford the nun an opportunity to give Martha more music lessons; her congregation also taught in the parish of Kenora, and Martha would be able to play the organ as often as she wanted.

The night following her long conversation with Sister Suzanne, Martha had been unable to sleep more than three hours. Early in the morning, seeing the pile of blankets and pillows on the floor, her mother was convinced Martha had to get away from Saint-Boniface. Assured her departure would be kept secret, Martha left, torn at the thought of giving in to Doris who would steal her boyfriend.

Approaching Kenora, Martha was struck by the many Indian faces she saw on the streets. On the 5th of January, the eve of Epiphany, she went downtown, on the pretence of doing some shopping, when, in fact, she was hoping to find her father. The majority of men looked downtrodden; the women seemed lost and depressed. If she crossed an Indian who resembled her father the least little bit, her heart skipped a beat; she slowed down and stared at him. She imagined Norman Star behind the seamed face, sickly complexion, belaboured or staggered gait, or the full head of still jet-black hair.

She sat at a table in a corner of a restaurant, watching Indians. Facing her, on the left, a man alone, two or three sweaters one on top of the other, buttons all askew, a fur cap held together with string. A stream of saliva ran down the corner of his lips. With each sip of coffee, he cast an accusing glance at Martha. What have you done to your father? His dry wrinkled skin gave him the appearance of a half-starved homeless wretch. No warm house for the poor bum, no nicely prepared meal, no clean clothes, no job to boost his self-esteem. Only two reproachful eyes... what have you done to your father?

Martha allowed the flow of accusations to invade her being, not even trying to justify her behaviour. Now a student at the Academy, she had almost forgotten her father; she had gone so far as to wish for a well-mannered, well-spoken father, a lawyer, or a doctor, perhaps.

Why was Norman Star nothing more than a clone of the Indian she saw before her now? If her usually rich imagination had invented the scenario of her father paying her a surprise visit, she would have quickly pushed it out of her mind; she would be ashamed of her father if he dared come to the Academy. Today, sitting opposite an Indian who was analyzing her features, she felt as if she had slapped her father across the face, branding him as a criminal. Ever since her arrival in Kenora, she was haunted by her incapacity to do anything for the one who had given her life.

For years she had ignored the fact that her nationality set her apart form girls "of good families;" now her knowledge allowed her to read reactions to her in people's faces. It would be so simple to change her name, change cities, to become anonymous somewhere, to take on a new identity, to move among White people. The more she stared at the Indian, this cold January day, the more she wished to rid herself of the roots impeding her progress.

She had heard of "the dirty Indians" who died in large numbers of tuberculosis because of their alcoholism and lack of hygiene. This form of racism, sustained by Whites, was common belief in these surroundings. Her classmates invited her less and less; and on a rare occasion when she agreed to join a group, she knew they had invited her through condescension and pity, when they really wished she would refuse. It was her fate: snobbish girls looked down their noses at her. Her first dates with Robert had been great until she realized people were attracted to him, not her.

In her imagination she reviewed the past and tried to map the future. An Indian woman got up and walked out of the restaurant. A teenager, who had been observing the woman for some time, made a comment, setting the whole gang off into gales of laughter. Martha was indignant. Was this the answer to her questions? She had decided: she would change her name... Yes, this was the end of Martha Star in Manitoba where the Métis didn't stand a chance...

However, her decision lacked substance: she needed better arguments to betray her own people. Was she destined to repeat her father's error? He had adopted the White man's ways and married a White woman, hoping to be more successful; he had rejected his family, convinced that turning his back on the reserve would facilitate his acceptance in the "civilized" world. And where was he now? Wandering aimlessly in Nowhere, Saskatchewan, or Alberta? If she hadn't insisted her mother place him in a care centre, he might still be in Winnipeg... She blamed herself for her father's desertion: he must have overheard her speaking of the White man's institution where they planned to send him.

In her imagined future, could Martha be luckier in spite of her Indian features? She was hesitant to give up her studies to go off on her own, at seventeen, in an unknown part of the world. She asked for another coffee, annoyed at not being able to order her life right there and then, and walked out of the restaurant and up the street along the row of shops. The church where she had played the organ the previous Sunday appeared as a haven. She wondered if she should go in. Praying might anaesthetize her mind. It was a joyous time of the year: she would think of her father, her mother alone among strangers; then there was Robert...

Inside, the crèche was lit up; they turned the lights off only at supper time. Martha went forward, sick at heart and unable to think clearly, the word "Métis" pounding in her head. Of course it was her Métis blood that made her a victim of Doris' arrogance and Robert's rejection. Why continue to fight in an unequal battle? Leaving was the only solution to her despair. And then, what if? Martha was so confused. If only they turned off the lights so she could cry her heart out.

The Baby Jesus, smiling with outstretched arms, is way too white. On the other hand, her attention is drawn to the two Wise Men—the dark-skinned and the yellow-skinned— the sacristan has just placed at the entrance to the stable. Colour and charm for Epiphany! How cute! If everyone on the planet was the same colour, the world would be a dull place. Each race is unique: rich with its own culture, language and tradition. Who said White people were superior? Martha looked closely at the two Wise men from the East: attractive and richly attired with their gold crowns and fabulous presents. She rested her elbows on the communion rail, and holding her head in both hands, she sighed and her mind was still. She remained there for a long while, until the sacristan tapped her on the shoulder and whispered: "It's closing time." Emerging from an almost hypnotic state, Martha stood up proudly and looked intently at the Wise Men. No, it's not right to associate knowledge, talent and success with the White race, and ignorance, defeat and poverty with the Indians. Every individual carries within himself the seeds of success.

And what if she held her head high and remained Martha Star without trying to please the Robert Lavallées of the world? What if she proclaimed her identity with confidence and pride? What if she got interested in the history and problems of the Métis people? What if she found a job to serve her people? What if, and this was the hardest "what if,» she found her father to soothe her conscience? Martha was astonished to discover inside herself so many questions leading to the challenge of finding her father. She felt a calm coming over her.

The next day, she played the organ at the Epiphany service; Sister Suzanne was by her side, smiling contentedly as she considered the deft fingers of a talented musician.

Back in Saint-Boniface, Martha was again haunted by thoughts of Robert. How could she possibly forget him when each time she went down to the basement, she had to pass the room where he had stayed after her mother moved in? And the letter, full of tender and passionate revelations, which, unbeknownst to him, she had now committed to memory. Martha feared her own imagination, the possibility of giving in to the power of her passion. Her whole life could be ruined by one small mistake, by blowing up harmless incidents. She was still tortured by the desire to get her revenge. Had she become blind to the facts? Or was she too hurt to think straight?

Martha recalled the day she ran away, the night Doris arrived, her spite, and the long hours she lay awake. The night before she left for Kenora, she had gone down to the basement, burning with desire, wanting to slide into Robert's bed and into his arms. That night she had decided to admit her feelings for him if only to steal him from the beautiful Doris.

Having become aware of her lust for him, she would offer him her body to regain his love. Once she was pregnant, he would marry her right away; they both loved children, and knew one another's thoughts on the matter.

Driven by her desire, she was about to open the door, when she paused to think of the two other women sleeping peacefully, unaware she was about to make a terrible mistake. They wouldn't have understood her foolish behaviour; the thought of their silent reproach upset her. Martha turned around and went back to her room.

For a few moments she stood with her back to the wall, her hand over her mouth, stifling her sobs; she managed to control herself, and fell into bed without getting under the covers; she didn't want to sleep; she only hoped to calm her despair. Sadly, she came up with only two choices: escape or seduction.

"I was right to go to Kenora to take my mind off things," Martha said out loud, as she sat down to read over the last paragraph of Robert's letter. "Martha, when two people are happy together, sad when they are apart, anxious to see one another again, able to share joys and failure, respectful of the other person's likes and dislikes, it's because they love one another. Please remember the wonderful times we spent together, the decisions we took together to help both our mothers, the encouragement we gave one another to study harder, and tell me if we can part without hurting one another terribly?"

Martha sighs deeply, lips trembling, looking longingly at the window where she can see the covering of snow, a sweet reminder of the snowshoe adventures with Robert. She would like to believe all the signs of tenderness directed to her, but the hurt is too great.

Once again she returned to her plan; she could get a job at the end of June and finish her grade twelve by correspondence. If she stayed in Manitoba, who could stop her from following Sister Suzanne's clever plan? Time would erase Robert from her life. As for Madame Lavallée, who insisted on mediating between Robert and herself, she would keep her distance and gradually sever ties. The day the sick woman had walked for the first time and asked to phone Robert, Martha's first impulse had been to refuse. However, the lady and her son had been so kind to her and her mother, looking after their every need, and refusing all gratitude; Martha swallowed her pride. And of course, Robert's letter was so full of warm, thoughtful words...

When they called him, Robert had been so excited at the other end of the line. He talked a mile a minute, trying to say as much as possible in the least possible time... asking for his mother, then Martha, and going from one to the other...

"Thank you for calling me, Martha," he said quietly and calmly. "Now I'll be able to concentrate on my studies. Thank you. I love you, I love you, I love you. Tell me you love me, too."

But the line was dead.

Eleven

Supported by Luke Jones and Paul Courchesne, Norman Star went down the narrow stairway, as light-hearted as a paper kite.

At the wheel of the old jalopy, Luke started humming: "It's a long way to Tipperary, it's a long way to go..." In the back seat, Paul took an old guitar and followed with: "For he's a jolly good fellow..." Norman smiled. The three were running away from a "civilization" that had destroyed the dreams of their youth. Winnipeg! The city of lights concealed its slums at night, but by day, its wounds were visible in the bright sunshine, brighter than anywhere else in Canada.

"You'll see, Norman," said Paul, "we'll live out in the open and eat fresh fish for a while. Then, we'll hunt, and in winter set some traps."

"But where are we going?" asked Norman.

"North," Paul and Luke replied.

In Selkirk, they dropped in on Luke's aunt. Weeds abounded all around the dilapidated shack; dead leaves piled up between the warped planks of the verandah and in the eaves troughs overflowing with dirt. New growth sprouted everywhere, rallying forces for a siege war.

Inside, a row of vials on the shelf of the bay window contained juices of dry roots and boiled leaves used to make poultices. The medicine woman examined Norman closely and asked him to follow her into a room furnished with benches, two wretched beds and huge crates used as wardrobes. She gave him a few bottles, forbade him to drink alcoholic beverages and even offered to look after him herself to ensure his recovery. She stated firmly Norman did not have cancer.

The patient hesitated before refusing the Indian woman; she reminded him of his grandmother—same gestures, same accent, same genuine concern. That evening the three Indians slept in the attic full of containers, bags of old cloths, and spider webs. Luke and Paul fell asleep as soon as they hit the pillow, and started to snore, "coming and going," while Norman fought the vermin seeking the warmth of his feverish body. Exasperated, he got up off the floor and turned on the light to find mice feasting on their cheese. The sight was disgusting. He was shivering, thinking of his princess' white body and clean sheets. In any case, he shared his friends' notion of going north, to enjoy wide open spaces, fresh air and FREEDOM.

The following day they pooled their resources to buy gas and reached Winnipeg Beach, a summer resort where the cottages were boarded up for winter. The three friends sighed nostalgically. How sweet it would be to stay in Winnipeg Beach until spring! What could be nicer than ice fishing with a few dogs and a sled!

They continued their journey, wondering why these White people needed a house, an RV, a boat and a vehicle. Every lot was filled to capacity; there was no room to move an inch on those little islands dedicated to human inhabitation, from Sans-Souci and Matlock to Ponemah and Winnipeg Beach. The homes of the rich were veritable castles hidden away in what used to be wilderness, the former Garden of Eden of the Redskins who lived in peace under the protection of the Great Manitou, the god who speaks on the vast lake.

"This place is too close to Winnipeg," Paul remarked; "we wouldn't be safe, here. Let's go to Camp Morton. Father Dubois will give us something to eat and a place to sleep."

"Norman is tired. He just threw up," Luke announced.

"I can keep going," Norman protested in a weak voice. "I want to see Father Dubois, too."

In Camp Morton, the priest greeted his former students with surprise and a great deal of reservation. Nevertheless he allowed them to spend a week in barracks on the air base. Generous meals in the mess, the cheerful company of recruits, and peaceful nights restored to Norman some of his strength, but his silence was a cause for concern. Where were they going anyway, and to find what?

"You were unwise to leave on this adventure with a sick man," Father Dubois remarked to Luke and Paul.

"It was so pitiful when he asked us to take him along. We shouldn't have told him we were leaving," Paul admitted sheepishly.

"What about his wife and daughter? He left without saying anything?"

"He thought they would be glad to get rid of him," replied Paul, as embarrassed as if he were speaking of himself.

"Listen both of you," the Oblate Father ordered. "Do you want to work? They're thinking of painting the barracks. I can have a word with the maintenance officer. I suppose you need money? Are you as lazy as ever?" he added, laughing loudly.

The two men were not amused. There was a long enigmatic silence when the priest expected them to give in. It was an attractive offer for two men who had nothing but debts. On the other hand, it wasn't fair to let Norman stagnate in the infirmary. After all, they had promised him he would get better faster with them than with the medicine woman and her vials.

"Paul, you take my car," Luke decided, "and go ahead with Norman. Find us a place to spend the winter. In the meantime, I'll make a bit of money and share it with you."

"Okay. We'll leave tomorrow," Paul replied. "You can come and visit us some time."

In the evening, Norman went looking for the priest. He spoke at length about his youth and disappointments. According to Father Dubois, who concluded Norman was on the verge of a nervous breakdown, the Indian had had a good life.

"I didn't wish for very much," said Norman. "A job in a garage and a car. You know, Father, in Winnipeg, with the Pères Oblats, I was happy. If Gisèle and Martha had got used to the Indians... Now I'm embarrassed to live with them and I want to die among my own people; not in a White man's hospital."

Around midnight, Father Dubois asked:

"Norman, is there anything else you want to tell me before you go?"

"Yes," answered Norman, hanging his head.

Inspired by the faith of his childhood, the grown man knelt before Father Dubois and made a list of his sins, in order to whiten his soul, as the Fort Alexander missionaries had taught him.

Very early the next day, they left Luke with Father Dubois and drove towards the west shore of Lake Winnipeg. In Riverton, Norman and Paul stopped, and discreetly went around the village, finding it all but deserted. They understood why when they read a poster advertising the Icelandic Festival in Gimli.

The two Indians walked along the river. At nightfall, they found shelter in a barn in the middle of a huge corn field. The night was cool. Norman, wide awake and nervous, started to regret his flight; he suffered acute pain in his back and stomach and was obliged to take a few drops of the precious "medicine" from Paul's backpack. It seemed as if death was hovering in their shelter beaten by wind and rain in the autumn night. Norman, lying against the door post, roof beams, hay and farm machinery spinning around him, perceived a magnificent husky coming towards him. The dog, in search of affection, looked at him with tender eyes, pushed his cap off, and licked his dry face. Norman felt the moist caresses on his neck and came back to his senses.

"You're beautiful," said Norman, putting his scrawny arms around its neck.

He rested his head against the dog's warm face, he stroked the gaunt body and wavy tail, hugging the white life-giving vision.

When the men left in the early hours of the morning, the dog followed them to their car parked at the entrance to the village, near the plaque to Sigtryggur Jonasson, named Father of Monday, and leader of the first contingent of Icelanders to arrive in Manitoba, in 1875. The two travellers admired a huge boat moored near the shore, glowing in the reflection of Lake Winnipeg. Since the discovery of mercury in certain species of fish, the government had banned commercial fishing in the lake. Meanwhile, the fishermen were anxious to start working again; most of them had no other means of livelihood.

In the midst of the Icelandic colony, Norman and Paul were strangers, intruders even. Their dark skin, black hair, and high cheek bones set them apart from the rosy-skinned, blond-maned giants.

"Look at him in the car," said Paul, pointing to the dog.

"It's a her," Norman corrected.

"Are we taking her with us?"

"I can't see why not. She's a stray."

"What are you going to call her?"

"I don't know."

"Let's call her Hecla," Paul suggested.

"Hecla? Whatever for?"

"That's where we're going. Hecla, a ghost village on Hecla Island."

"An island in the lake?" Norman was delighted.

Bounding from the back seat, the dog leaped to the front and took her place between the passengers. Her friskiness gave new courage to the two Indians who were beginning to get a little nervous about their destination.

"Tell me about Hecla," said Norman, "the village, not the dog."

"Hecla is the largest island in Lake Winnipeg; it's also a provincial park. About thirty Icelandic families took homesteads there in 1876 and called it Hecla, after a volcano in Iceland. My mother comes from there; she told me about this. The owner of the sawmill, who had an Icelandic wife, taught the settlers how to fish through the ice the Indian way."

They drove along the shore of the clear majestic lake; flocks of aquatic birds squawked in the blue sky. Earth, sky, vegetation, water—a wild, bewitching panorama. It made one want to find a place in this strange but friendly territory. Unfortunately, Norman was getting tired; the trip came to an end when the car ran out of gas.

They wouldn't be able to cross to their island before Wednesday; the ferry went only twice a week. Disappointed and hungry, the two Indians were too shy to knock at a nearby house; they had just decided to sleep in their car when the ferry-driver, a Métis, invited them to spend the night at his house.

It was clean, and his wife was shy but friendly. While Norman rested and the children played with Hecla, Paul watched Mrs. Sinclair making bannock. He remembered how, as a child, he loved to sink his little brown hands in the dough his mother kneaded and take huge bites out of the golden crust. The housewife answered his question. You need six cups of flour, a half pound of fat, a teaspoon of butter, a teaspoon of salt, and if you have some, a little oil so the dough doesn't stick to your hands.

Mrs. Sinclair divided the dough in four parts, and gave one to Paul so he could try his hand at kneading. Then they let the dough stand, kneaded it again; it was left to stand again, and kneaded a third time. Finally, they pricked it with a fork in several places to let the air in, and put it in a hot oven. Paul was excited at the idea of making bannock in their own shack.

The hot bread in the middle of the table had a magical effect. Bannock! The Indians and Métis' own bread. Here on the peaceful prairie, in the clean air of someone's home, surrounded by people who liked them, Paul and Norman smiled. Here, respectful of God and Nature, people opened their hearts to the poor, the wanderer, the sick, even the Indian.

"Paul," whispered Norman, from his home-made pine bed, "I'd like to stay here. I know I could get better."

"Wait till you see Hecla Island. You'll never want to go back to Winnipeg."

That night, Norman dreamed of freedom with Gisèle and Martha. Twice he woke up in a sweat; each time he put an arm out to stroke the dog; her coat was silky smooth from hours of grooming, courtesy of the children.

Twelve

On Hecla Island, they found the antidote to Main Street, the noisy artery forever vomiting its hellish racket. Deep in unspoiled nature, a silent path welcomed new footsteps, echoing the joyous crunching of fragile plants.

"The trees are small here," Paul and Norman observed.

"Because of the cold," explained Laurent Sinclair. He was only eighteen years old and proud to share his knowledge with the Winnipeggers.

His father had allowed him to spend the week on the island; he was ecstatic, as he would have followed Paul to the ends of the earth. Hearing Paul play modern and Western tunes, he dreamed of playing the guitar himself. Although the guitar is one of the most difficult instruments to master, he felt he could do it. His dream took flight; he protected it during the day, but freed it at night, captured it again, and caged it to better nourish and sustain it. First chance he had, he would talk to Paul about it.

Meanwhile, he walked energetically, inspecting the surroundings, ready to shoot if a wild animal crossed their path. Norman and Paul followed their guide, free to delight in the greens, yellows and browns of the scenery before them. Norman, preferring drawing, had neglected his math and science courses in school, considering them as boring as rainfall. Spotting the red-osier dogwood covered with berries, then the pembina and the hazelnut, the three men paused a moment to feast on the generosity of the wilderness, then continued on their way, much revived.

"When you get to the large spruce by the lake, take a right," announced Laurent who was bringing up the rear. "The abandoned house is a few yards away."

Suddenly an unusual sound broke out, stopping the men dead in their tracks. Songs, noises and cries announced a celebration in the clearing. The sounds went "boom, boom, boo, boom, boom, boo," in quick succession.

"A dance," exclaimed Laurent, identifying the sounds he had heard his grandfather mimic. "They're prairie chickens."

"The dance of the prairie chickens?"

"Yes, they dance twice a year."

The young Métis listened closely and pointed west.

"Quick, this way," he said mysteriously.

"No, this way," argued Paul softly, pointing in a different direction.

"No. I'm certain," Laurent insisted.

Paul was impressed by Laurent's excellent hearing; he was sorry he had lost the gift of his race. Nature had become a stranger to him; she was getting her vengeance since he had abandoned her for city pavements.

A strange buzzing rose from everywhere and nowhere, filling the forest with sound; it was punctuated by piercing shrieks of "caw, caw!"

"The chickens!" Laurent cried once again. "The cocks go *Boom, Boo-oo,* and the hens answer *Caw, Caw.*"

The Métis lad did an excellent imitation of the cries of both males and females: his companions were flabbergasted.

"The dance is about to begin," said Laurent, like a priest announcing the start of holy mass.

Along the stream, hundreds of hens, in single file, flapped their wings; heads low, they chased one another in mad pursuit. Their "onomatopoeia" continued, broken by the louder cry of the cocks, in two-part counterpoint.

"They look mad. Look at them spinning. They're bewitched," said Norman.

"That's true; now, if I wanted, I could kill dozens of them because nothing disturbs them. My grandfather said killing chickens during their dance brings bad luck."

"To shoot them during their hysterics would be a cowardly deed," added Norman.

Lying on his stomach in the dew, eyes glued on the primitive ballet, Paul imagined a choreography inspired by this phenomenon. Suddenly he wanted to start a new life on mysterious Hecla Island. Once his father had come here to act as a guide to an American hunter; and this is where he had met his wife.

Like the people of his reserve, he refused to hunt, fish, or trap; consequently, he knew nothing of the secret life of prairie animals. In the solitude of the North, prairie chickens still danced, but for how much longer? What if ignorant hunters exterminated them? Laurent guessed Paul wanted to know more about the chickens, and continued solemnly:

"The prairie chicken dance occurs one more time in spring: whenever the weather is fine, from the end of March to the middle of June. And again from the end of August to the end of November. After the dance the cocks and hens scatter about to mate. That's the fun part. But we don't have to worry, they'll dance again next year. The hens will produce hundreds of baby cocks and hens."

Paul and Norman felt a tremor in their groin, proof their male instincts had not abandoned them. The former thought of his wife who had left him; the latter of Gisèle whom he hadn't touched for so long.

Rather moved, the two Indians stood up after witnessing the almost sacred ritual, beset by a powerful need for a woman. In Winnipeg Norman had given up thinking he could win Gisèle back, while Paul had been rejected by the women he desired. Frustration seemed to have aged the former Fort Alexander guitarist, who, because he felt he was still attractive, refused to accept that women no longer fell for him gratis, and to engage in rental love .

One night, in a Winnipeg bar, he had pinched a pretty waitress' bum, to hear insults. Dirty Indian! He would always be an Indian, in spite of his efforts to behave and dress like a White man. In Hecla, there must be women. Paul was only in his thirties; he wasn't about to stagnate in Hecla for the rest of his days; he only wanted to give Norman a chance.

The long narrow building about to become lodgings for the two Winnipeg Indians had never known the strokes of a paint brush. it was built of squared tree trunks one on top of the other, with dovetailed corners, and a chimney made of chinked poles inside a huge beam. Laurent stepped inside and immediately lit a fire for heat and light.

"Wait," said Laurent. "Before you get settled, I have a surprise."

He went to a corner, and spread out a superb buffalo hide, and dragged it in front of the crackling fire. The dog barked, and jumped back and forth, crawled from side to side, ready to take off if this dark flat beast came to life. Finally, she calmed down, reassured by the sight of the three men stretched out on the rug, laughing and enjoying the furry warmth.

"The skin belonged to my great-grandfather," said Laurent. "My father leaves it here; he uses it when he comes hunting in fall or trapping in wintertime."

The fur, the smell of the supple skin, the warmth of the hair, reminded the Indians of delicious buffalo meat they had tasted once, during a centenary celebration hosted by White people. Father Letendre had managed to get for his musicians a few pieces of meat which was now a rare treat in Manitoba.

Lolling in front of the bright fire, the campers drank tea and ate Madame Sinclair's bannock, spread with gobs of butter. Outside, frogs chatted and cheered the arrival of the new residents.

Lit by the flames, doors, window, floor, and ceiling appeared artistically sculpted from quality materials. The next day, the visitors discovered night had transformed the most trivial objects... They found a wooden bucket for collecting water, a water skin, a cast-iron kettle, a pine table and benches, two shelves from which hung a deerskin. A real museum!

The first night, Norman hardly slept, his heart heavy with thoughts of a possible recovery, and his need to quench his thirst for freedom. The moon greeted him from its perch, and stars twinkled through the little window. They wished to be admired... or else, make a pact with the one they wished to detain on Hecla Island. But where was his own star?

He had voiced his concerns to Mrs. Sinclair regarding food and medicine, and expressed his fear there would be no doctor or priest to assist him at his final hour; she had simply replied:

"You'll eat venison, dried or smoked fish, bannock and berries; I'll teach you to fend for yourself. And if you get sick, I'll bring you over here."

The silence of the night was broken only by a wood owl hooting, a coyote moaning, or the cackling of hens pursued by untiring cocks. Hecla sat up on her hind legs, ears trembling; she lay down again on her side, paws outstretched, her nose resting on Norman's legs, her heart at peace. She was nervous, and shifted her position from time to time; finally she got up and lay with her back curved into the hollow of Norman's tummy.

In this natural temple, assisted by Paul, Laurent and Hecla, Norman's battle against death, his tyrannical Winnipeg mistress, was almost sweet. He idled for hours on end, enveloped by the tepid wind from the lake, ate hungrily, and slept. Unlike on Main Street, he had no use for his sleeping pills. Hecla! Island of bright sunshine, clean water and healthy food; the sky kept her secret. Far from Winnipeg, the sick man drew closer to those who had tried to teach him the customs and beliefs of his ancestors.

That year, the sun stayed on through October and November. The superstitious residents attributed the unusually warm weather to the coming of the Indians. But what exactly were they doing in Hecla?

Thirteen

Autumn was short that year; they stayed out only two evenings. The house was near a swamp and healthy mosquitoes formed a mobile army attacking the city-dwellers, while silent frogs circled their feet. They made thick smoke to chase the blood-sucking pests; then, from time to time, one of them got up to counter-attack. Like a hockey player, armed with a broom, he counted shots, hitting any amphibian too heavy to escape. Later, Norman felt strangely quiet, rocked to sleep by the sound of Paul's music. Paul, the romantic, was forever plucking or scraping the strings of his guitar, usually the measure of his moods.

When the cold started to seep through the long boards, Paul became more taciturn. Winter frightened him, drove him mad. He imagined snow banks blocking the windows and roof of the house. Some days he went so far as to think they would leave by the upper windows, for the building was totally exposed to whatever merciless blizzard that chose to descend upon them. Never before had Paul felt such solitude. He missed his Main street pals, the movies shown in "their cinemas," the bars filled with unemployed men, the daily pilgrimage to the bus station to beg for cigarettes. One day, when Laurent came to bring them old clothes, he declared:

"I'm bored here. I want to leave this place."

"Look, you can't leave. Norman is eating better. He's even gained some weight. If you want to save him, you have to survive the winter in Hecla."

"I'd like to go and see Luke in Camp Morton."

"Wait. I came here today with a proposal."

Paul was delighted with Laurent's suggestion. No more evenings with Norman who retired at seven o'clock; no more empty hours of quiet so as not to disturb Norman. Mr. Sinclair's idea was great; he wanted to use his winter camp. The two Indians could stay in the village, in one of the houses on the road next to the lake. They talked most of the night. Paul was pleased: he could return to civilization, and Laurent's wish would be granted.

Paul and Norman settled into a grey shingled building, surrounded by yellowish grass kept alive here and there by a radiant sun. Two doors in front, two identical windows on the left side, another on the right, and a circular window in the gable. On one side, two openings side by side indicated the Sinclairs had enlarged their house twice before abandoning it for a more comfortable one. The men had separate rooms; even the dog would live like a queen in her own space at the back of the house.

Very soon a little community formed in the newcomers' tiny house on the island. Parents were thankful for their presence in the hamlet. The Sinclairs had managed to gather four violins, a set of drums, a banjo and three guitars. The parents admitted Paul and Norman played well, and paid Mr. Sinclair's suggested price for lessons. Saturday and Sunday became feast days in the old house: the little orchestra practiced, the instructors listening attentively to the piece each one studied during the week. The students were obviously improving, even though their impatience often upset the teachers, who were by nature rather nonchalant. The budding musicians wanted to play in the Christmas concert and for their schoolteacher's wedding in February. Norman was annoyed by their attitude: by mid-December he would have heard the same songs a thousand times over. Paul was determined not to see the break-up of the promising little band, and suggested Norman spend more time painting and drawing; he would be forced to go out, walk by the lake, and linger there to sketch. So the little urchins could continue plucking and scraping strings, real music to Paul's ears.

Norman still wondered if he was truly an artist, or if this was just an idle dream. He had often lingered near art shops in Winnipeg, attracted by the displays of material. But he had never had enough courage to go inside. He longed to touch the papers, handle the brushes or colour pencils. He had come so close to buying something, just to satisfy his fantasy. Can an uncultured Indian do such a thing? Only the well-to-do can ever be artists, right? Who can be a genius? White people?

In Hecla he could paint in the open. His pockets were already bulging with sketches drawn on the backs of match books Paul had discarded. He bought a charcoal pencil, black ink, and art paper at the general store. The Icelandic clerk had a brother who was a commercial artist in Winnipeg. She could advise him and order what he needed.

From now on, he would pursue his favourite hobby... for once he would be happy doing what he loved. Happiness! Was it possible? Why not? After all he was a free man living in a healthy place; his health was improving: he went out every day, abstained from alcohol and tobacco, and faithfully took the medicine from the Selkirk medicine woman.

He was tortured by the thought he had abandoned Gisèle—he should have made her happy. As for Martha, the memory of her frank, intelligent face recalled his indignity, his betrayal. But he would immediately retract: "No, I had become a burden to them, a barrier to a normal life among French Canadians."

His failure had made him decide to move to different surroundings to start a new life. Father Dubois had not condemned him for running away. Before going to the general store, Norman made an inventory of his sketches scattered here and there; then, quick as a wink, grasping the significance of his samples, he gave each one a title and a number, and placed them contentedly in an empty cigar box. He counted fifty-four drawings. Fifty-four times ever since the government doctor had told him his lungs were better than his own, he had tried to immortalize the face of his loved ones, to capture bits of the life he was trying to hang on to.

His collection included sceneries—a sunrise and a moonscape—the hull of an old fishing boat, the fishmonger's ice wagon, the chapel, the school, Gisèle and Martha, Mrs. Sinclair, John, the forest warden, and Hecla, his faithful companion in his quest for creative ideas. Without realizing it, he had created an impressive bank of topics; he paid no attention to a slowly emerging style, but discovered nonetheless the secrets of objects, and the souls of the living models had caught his artist's eye. That day, Norman Star, the Main Street Indian, felt he had lost his lifeless expression and halting speech.

DECEMBER TWENTIETH. Mr. Sinclair opened the sliding doors separating the two classrooms for the traditional Christmas concert. For the occasion, the parents stacked the desks in the garage and raised a platform concealed behind Mrs. Sinclair's clean white sheets. The walls were adorned with spruce branches giving off the most wonderful scent; in the moist greenery nestled artificial icicles, flowers, and ornaments.

At the last minute Luke arrived with the Camp Morton chaplain, and the audience was suddenly silent. The two guests of honour were astonished to see the audience rise to greet them with obvious respect. Norman, at the piano, tackled a rousing "We wish you a Merry Christmas." The audience listened attentively; heads rose, then a few voices led the singing, followed by the more timid voices, some out of tune, all joining in the lively melody. They sang for Father Dubois, straight from the heart, whether Icelandic, Métis, German, Ukrainian. Indian, or French Canadian; the carol carried its message of fraternity and love. The concert followed the Plains tradition: songs, pantomimes, and skits, all in a festive atmosphere. The schoolteacher ignored the awkward gestures or slips of memory.

"The school orchestra, under the direction of Paul Courchesne and Norman Star," announced Laurent Sinclair with a heavy Métis accent.

Norman was touched by Laurent's address; he lavished praise on the musician and the effectiveness of his leadership. They had a secret: Norman had convinced Laurent he was more talented for the piano, so Laurent agreed to give up the guitar.

Applause broke out when the "curtain" rose; there were nine little musicians: eyes wide, fidgeting nervously, mouths open, concentrating on the task at hand. They wore black trousers, white shirts and bright red sashes. The highlight of the evening featured Pall Erlendson on drums! He was fabulous! Such a delightful little guy, face flushed, a shock of blond hair in his eyes, pudgy arms beating the air, and short legs dancing on the pedals. For the fiddle solos the audience kept a solemn silence.

Paul had an incredible repertoire: "Jingle Bells," "Rudolph the Red-Nosed Reindeer," "The Drummer Boy," "Holy Night," etc. While his musicians caught their breath in the hot school room, Paul played with gusto, accompanied by the beating of shoes on the oiled floor. The Manitoba wind had never before carried such merry echoes.

Father Dubois' favourite piece, "Les anges dans nos campagnes," was coming to an end when a crashing noise stopped Paul short, hands lifted high above the damp keyboard. Was the roof falling in? No, there was laughter, and it became general as members of the audience in turn saw the cause of the racket. They laughed so hard they couldn't relate the incident, and the rest merely got caught up in the general hilarity.

Indeed, it was big Jos. Sigurdson, who had sneezed so hard his chair had collapsed under him. His huge mass had crushed the bottle hidden in his coat pocket. Now his head bathed in the precious liquid. The uninitiated guessed it was rye, the connoisseurs argued scotch; in any case even those with less educated noses laughed till their sides split.

This comic incident turned out to be the surprise number at the Hecla Christmas concert. At the end of the evening, they were still teasing big Jos., who, far from humiliated by the incident, declared the strong odour from the flask had deodorized the gases that had escaped from his rear end when he sneezed.

The evening would provide another event long remembered by the inhabitants of Hecla. Until a half hour past midnight, Norman Star, Paul Courchesne and Luke Jones accompanied the dancing; reels, Western and popular tunes. Even Father Dubois, elegant and fleet-footed, had joined in to give the prettiest island girls a spin. That evening the Indians' house was renamed The Musicians' House.

However, only two days afterwards, bad news broke out: Paul had left the island with Father Dubois. Too shy to make his decision known, he had departed without ceremony; but he had agreed to use his musical talent to serve the army reserves in Camp Morton.

Luke returned to Winnipeg, as his alcohol problem had worsened; he hadn't saved any money in spite of the advantage he enjoyed or Father Dubois' efforts to set him straight. Norman, feeling puzzled, undecided, and sympathetic towards his childhood friend, had tried to convince him to stay. But Luke was unwilling to go into exile in an even more northerly location.

"Your Hecla Island is too far and too cold," he replied. "Besides, you wouldn't let me have a drink. Total abstinence."

"Poor Luke! What will you do in Winnipeg?"

"Don't worry. In Winnipeg, I'll have a welfare cheque," Luke laughed.

At a time when Norman was seeing a light at the end of his tunnel, his Hecla companion was abandoning him, and Luke was giving him second thoughts about Winnipeg. Would he remain alone in Hecla, or would he go back south and risk seeing Gisèle and Martha again?

Fourteen

Gisèle liked this Québécois who smiled at her whenever they met on Aulneau Street. One day he approached her for a friendly conversation about the weather; then, gazing intently at her he suggested he would like to get acquainted. A jovial fellow with a keen sense of humour, he found it difficult to spend a quiet week-end; he had to go dancing, see a movie or eat in a restaurant. Solitude drove him crazy. He needed the therapeutic atmosphere of Winnipeg in order to survive the week in a narrow windowless office at the National Bank. He had no savings, and enjoyed spending every cent of his meagre salary.

"Why save?" he responded whenever someone expressed amazement at his nonchalance about the future. "Manitobans look grim because they live for tomorrow," he added with his characteristic Québec laugh.

Their meetings became gradually more frequent, and Gisèle was feeling attracted to this generous man who dressed rather elegantly. Their respective marriages had been failures, so they were cautious, not knowing if they still wanted the warmth of a home and a faithful heart.

Philippe Beaudoin's wife, a confirmed alcoholic, had become little more than a stray, a refugee at her daughter's, somewhere in the Eastern Townships of Québec. As for Gisèle, she didn't quite know what to make of Norman Star's disappearance. He might have committed suicide...

Norman's sudden departure had disturbed her greatly, but afterwards, a combination of circumstances alleviated her solitude. When she recalled the two stages of her life, her imagination rejected Gisèle Star, and the picture of Gisèle Bergevin dominated. She held out her hand to the woman she had been before her marriage; thus she was slowly being reborn to a new life where shone a glimmer of happiness.

Being with Philippe brought back memories of Québec, her happy childhood, her parents' affection. She felt younger, more natural and better adapted to her surroundings. They spoke with the same accent, recalling Québec and happier days: the brilliant autumn colours, the joys of winter in the mountains, the fun of maple sugar season in spring, and the warm sandy beaches. Gisèle often wondered what was the basis of her attraction to this man: Philippe himself or Québec.

The first time Martha met Philippe Beaudoin, she stopped worrying about her mother's future. Gisèle worked at the Saint-Boniface Hospital, and was paying the rent on her own apartment. "My mother doesn't have to bury herself alive because my father abandoned her," Martha thought. According to Madame Lavallée, a sweet, pretty, thirty-year old should have a circle of friends; and Gisèle wouldn't find one if she stayed with an invalid.

Furthermore, when Martha spoke of leaving, Lucille Lavallée insisted she stay, even though she was beginning to manage quite well with just a cleaning lady. "Three more weeks, and we'll put an end to the embarrassing situation between Martha and me, as soon as Robert comes back from Ottawa," Lucille repeated to herself.

Martha, too, felt uncomfortable, and rebelled at the thought of living under the same roof as Robert. She'd crawl in the dirt rather than humiliate herself. She was determined to forget Robert. The best way was to run away, turn the page, and start anew. Martha was seriously considering going to live in Winnipeg, and never again setting foot in Saint-Boniface; she had even gone to see various apartments on Edmonton and Palmerston streets, checked the bus routes, and made a tentative budget to see if she could afford a decent living.

Secretly, the young student lived another drama; she was overwhelmed with shame, in spite of positive efforts to crush it. She pushed out of her mind all thoughts of her runaway father, a real primitive, in the true meaning of the word, even though her memories of him evoked only profound goodness, boundless generosity, and absolute sincerity. She knew he had a big heart, yet she could no longer love him. What could be gained by seeing him again?

She felt unable to bring home other young people her age; they despised Indians and Métis. During their discussions in history class, they quickly categorized Indian people: they were lazy, fornicating drunkards. Outcasts! the dregs of society!

In some places, if they went to the same hotels as Whites, the glasses used to serve Indians were kept separate from those for "civilized" customers; in other places, the waiter opened the windows when they came in. Some drinkers changed tables if Indians sat next to them, trying to get away from offensive odours. In other establishments, Indian business was so lucrative the owners boasted of living off "those people" who were so easily intimidated. When they had had too much to drink, they were simply thrown out onto the street with no thought of how they would get home. Whatever the weather, the "dirty Indian" was simply booted out.

Martha couldn't rid herself of the dreadful images of Main Street: she relived the cries of terror, the pools of blood and vomit, the odours of alcohol and garbage. Nothing could make her go near her parents' old neighbourhood with its drunks and prostitutes. If she had to go on Main Street, she closed her eyes to the painful memories of her teenage years.

How had Martha come to this sudden change in attitude towards Native people? After insisting her mother spend all her savings to find the runaway, she realized her feelings had shifted; she could no longer commiserate over her sick father's misfortune, wherever he was, awaiting a solitary end. How much of her distress was due to her defeat at the hands of Robert's other girl friend? She did not know.

Martha found comfort in Madame Lavallée's progress and Robert's kind words. But she was unable to rid herself of her desire to get her revenge. Many times, she had bared her soul to find the reason for her spite. Was it a lovers' quarrel? Or was she feeling contempt for her own Indian blood? Both aspects were equally significant: the problem of the love affair, and the denial of her roots. She saw only one solution: she would sever ties with the Métis nation.

One day, seeing crab grass shrivelling to death from herbicide applied on someone's lawn, she had felt encouraged to go on. A few minutes later, she was with Sister Suzanne.

"This Doris Gardner, you really hate her, don't you?"

"She's so beautiful and elegant."

"But you're not like that, Martha. If physical appearance is the only thing Robert is interested in, you're not losing much. So don't fret. Can I say something? Maybe you should admit your share of responsibility in this affair. You lost your temper, and now you refuse to talk to him. He tried to explain. You've judged him before hearing him out."

Martha, already too proud to accept the uncertainty she found herself in, was not about to admit her wrongs. She decided then and there she would forget Robert.

A few days later, Claude Poitras invited her for the third time to go out to a movie.

Martha was able to convince herself he "was stuck on her;" furthermore she was about to show Madame Lavallée that Robert was not the only boy in Saint-Boniface.

"Do you want me to do your hair before supper?" Martha asked Madame Lavallée.

"Are you going out?" the lady answered, trying to sound indifferent

"Yes, I'm going out with Claude Poitras."

Lucille wished she could have spoken openly as she used to do before Doris' visit to Manitoba, but she had before her a stubborn little woman who had been hurt, usually silent, but on the verge of tears each time Robert's name was mentioned.

"Martha, have you decided if you are going to live with your mother? Oh! the water is too hot," Lucille complained.

"Sorry, I was thinking of something else." Madame Lavallée felt nervous tension in the hands vigorously rubbing her scalp.

"I'm sorry," Martha repeated. "How shall I do your hair?" she asked at once, eager to find a topic of conversation.

Claude Poitras' jaw dropped as he caught sight of Martha in the doorway. He announced his triumph with fanfare:

"I've got Dad's car. If you agree, we'll go to a couple of night clubs instead of staying in and listening to the crunching of popcorn."

"No, I'd rather not," said Martha, "I have an algebra exam tomorrow; if I want to think clearly..."

"Yeah, I understand. School, school, school. If you want my opinion, you study too much. You should go out more often—with me, of course—and study less. Listen to the advice of a future lawyer. Anyway, why not have fun? Life is so short."

The cinema was half empty, and the film, one of the most boring of the year. Claude had fun guessing the progression of the plot. Martha enjoyed his witty comments, concluding this teasing fellow was rather intelligent. After the film, they met Jacques Simard and Lyne Corbeil in the parking lot. As they were getting into their cars, they saw Marilou Simoneau and Gilles Caron coming towards them.

"Let's go to the club," suggested Jacques and Gilles. "It's a lot of fun."

"No, come to my house," Claude responded.

"Your house? Are you kidding? Can you imagine your mother with a gang of six in her living room? If you think we'll finish the evening in her presence, you're nuts," remarked Lyne Corbeil. She hated the stuffy Madame Poitras.

"*Le vieux* is out with *la vieille*."

"Why didn't you say so?" said Gilles with his nose in the air, and faking a British accent.

"What'll it be: rum, scotch, rye, gin?" Claude announced as he walked up the steps. "Poitras' bar opens in ten seconds."

They toasted much too soon. Less than a half hour had passed, and Martha and Claude were alone on the living room sofa. The other two couples were nowhere in sight. Where had they gone? In the room above, perhaps. They heard shoes drop on the floor, and, from down the hall on the main floor, they heard stifled chuckling.

Claude could think of nothing else to say about films or school. Embarrassed by the turn of events, he looked uneasy as Martha glanced at her watch. "She must think I'm boring and unsophisticated," he wondered, "if she's comparing me to Gilles and Jacques." Suddenly he drew the girl to him and kissed her crudely and disgustingly. Martha was aghast. His impatient hands crushed her breasts, and groped under her narrow skirt. Lying underneath a boy she no longer recognized, Martha thought of slapping his face; but she controlled herself and spit out:

"You bastard!"

"And you? A dirty Indian!" Claude replied in anger.

Martha gasped. Such a monumental insult from the mouth of a boy she thought was her new friend. She couldn't very well let him get his way. She had no intention of playing at love-making, much less arouse a male to lead him into having sex; she preferred Claude thought her a naive young thing. The same went for his friends on their first rendez-vous with Lyne and Marilou. Fuming and raging, eyes wild, face flushed, Martha shoved the limp body away from her and onto the floor. She jumped up, pulled her sweater back over her hips, looked at Claude with contempt, grabbed her handbag and her raincoat, and went to the telephone.

"No. don't. You're crazy. I just wanted to have fun. Sit down. We have to talk. Martha, forgive me. I lost control because I don't often have a drink, and tonight I drank too quickly. Anyway, I didn't want to look like a fool," he added sheepishly, motioning towards the ceiling and the next wall.

But the words "dirty Indian" were already in his head, thought Martha. She shrieked: "Stay away from me. There's nothing else to say."

Claude repeated his apologies, admitted he had acted like a bastard, a good-for-nothing; all for naught, nothing appeased Martha's anger. She stood before him, shifting from one foot to the other, wiping her tears, sighing impatiently, turning her back each time he came near her, and drawing back when he tried to touch her. Obviously contrite, Claude kept his hand on the telephone, begging forgiveness. She might forget the incident of the wandering hands, but never the words "dirty Indian" uttered with such disdain.

Martha wasn't listening, and didn't want to listen; she wasn't looking and didn't want to look at the boy she now hated; she had accepted his invitation so impulsively. Eleven thirty. Eleven forty-five. Midnight.

"I'm going home alone. I can walk. I don't need you."

"No, wait. I'll drive you." The five minutes in the car seemed like hours. Martha looked away from Claude, staring almost provocatively at the houses, shops, and lingering pedestrians. The boy searched for more words to add to his defence; he drove slowly, trying to muster enough courage to apologize one more time.

When the car stopped on Saint-Jean-Baptiste, Martha got out quickly; no thank you's for the movie, no good-night's; she slammed the door angrily. The message was clear. They were suddenly at opposite poles, all links between them severed forever.

The young girl, her face bathed in tears, threw her raincoat on a chair in the hallway, and dashed upstairs, gripping the banister so as not to trip. She opened the door without knocking, and, still trembling, snuggled against Lucille. She had been reading, hoping the girl might come in and chat. As she used to do when she told every detail of her least significant dates, Martha's sobs broke the silence of the night. Anger, conceit, distress and disappointment flowed along with the tears. Never before had she hungered to love and be loved as on this regrettable evening.

"Okay, little one, just you cry," said Lucille, tapping gently on her frail shoulders.

Martha cried torrents of tears; then the sobs were less frequent, lessened, then stopped. The fit of tears ended with a long sigh, like a summer breeze after a storm. Martha lay quietly now, but stayed in the same position, avoiding Lucille's gaze.

"Do you want to tell me about it, Martha?"

"Life is so cruel. I wish I was somewhere far away," Martha started sobbing again. "I hate Saint-Boniface."

"Come on, now. You feel this way now, but time will fix things. Your date with Claude didn't work out? He seemed so nice each time he came here. If you want to talk, Martha, I'm listening. I'm not sleepy tonight, and another short night won't do me any harm."

Martha was silent. Madame Lavallée understood the timing was wrong; it was better not to insist. In any case, she would have preferred talking about Robert who had just phoned. He first inquired about Martha, and said he wanted to make peace as soon as possible. The cold war between them was preventing him from concentrating on his studies. Lucille knew her son's character well enough: he was always reluctant to end a friendship, much less provoke resentment in another person.

Martha dozed off in Madame Lavallée's big bed. She would have loved to sleep here, just not to have to get up and find her sorrow had followed her to her own room. When Lucille offered her a place, Martha got undressed in a fraction of a second, and slid between the warm sheets with a smile of satisfaction.

When Robert came home, on the 3rd of May, Martha had moved to the Provencher Street convent to finish the last two months of school.

Fifteen

"They should ban final exams from the school system," thought Martha as she went to study hall. Determined to succeed, she was up at the crack of dawn, with the nuns. She hoped to get a job at the National Bank, with a recommendation from Philippe Beaudoin, her mother's friend. If anything went wrong she would have to cancel her grade twelve correspondence courses, and revoke her plans. In addition to academic subjects, Martha continued studying music, giving lessons to Sister Suzanne's beginners, and taking part in competitions and festivals. If she didn't obtain her grade eleven diploma, it was "Good-bye, Farewell" to all her dreams.

She would need good health and an excellent morale to get herself through the weeks of hard work and strict discipline she subjected herself to; she couldn't afford to go out or waste a second. The infirmary sister was concerned about the little emaciated face. Martha loved going to class, but exams terrified her. She lost her appetite, slept fitfully, and lost a lot of weight. Fortunately, she managed to keep up her spirits by thinking of next July and freedom; whenever she felt exhausted, the thought revived her. Indeed, she planned to take a few weeks' holidays before starting at the bank; she hoped to go swimming, cycling, and Sister Suzanne's parents had a cottage where she might spend some time.

Back in Saint-Boniface, Robert had phoned her four or five times to say "hello", to invite her to see his mother, or to play tennis. One day, unable to invent any more reasons to see her, he sounded off impatiently:

"Don't you understand? I want to see you. I'm anxious to speak to you."

"After final exams," Martha replied.

Satisfied with this promise, Robert, relatively busy with his regular job at the *Winnipeg Tribune*, waited patiently, hoping to be invited to the graduation dance. However, when he learned Jacques Laperrière was Martha's date, he was very angry at Martha for breaking her word.

Jacques was on his best behaviour, and Martha had a wonderful time. Unfortunately, there was after-grad. Ginette Mercure, unbeknownst to Martha, had invited "certain" friends to her parents' home to finish off the evening. Just imagine! Wellington Crescent!

The chosen few boasted about being invited. The Mercure home had twenty-two rooms and three fireplaces. It was decorated with oak panelling, paintings of well-known artists, magnificent staircases, luxurious carpets and furnishings; in short, it was a place the more modest young people only dreamed about.

In the evening, standing next to a doorway, Martha had watched Ginette Mercure's selected friends disappear inside. Jacques Laperrière, seeing her there, came towards her and announced sheepishly:

"Martha, excuse me, but I've been invited to Ginette's. I can pay a taxi to take you home. Ginette invited only a dozen people because... 'cause... well... I don't know, really. There, Lucien could take you home. He hasn't been invited either. You could finish the evening together. I wish Ginette had invited you, but I didn't dare suggest it. I'm just dying to go to the Mercure's. You understand, don't you?"

Of course, Martha understands. She understands only too well, the poor girl, staring at her little Woolworth's evening bag. She knows she carries with her the aura of the dispossessed, especially since money is getting scarce, and she can no longer count on Madame Lavallée to lend her an article of jewelry or buy her a new dress. Silent, she walks proudly towards the room adjoining the foyer. Fine, she'll finish the evening alone, seeing her date prefers the company of the well-to-do.

In the half-light, she dries her tears and dials a number. Waiting for an answer, she absent-mindedly peeks between the slats of the venetian blind. She can hardly believe her eyes! Ginette Mercure going down the front steps, Jacques' arms around her. Martha hears their laughter. They're probably making fun of her, no doubt taking great pleasure in having dumped her so easily.

Martha is paralyzed, her automatic responses frozen. She puts down the receiver and sits down slowly, waiting for her head to clear. She feels she's about to explode. Is this real? Her classmates are just occasional friends, snobs who talk to her only when they need her, but who pounce on her for any reason? Pale and trembling, she turns her back to the window. In her rage, she wants to destroy something, knock over the plush chairs in the hotel foyer, unfurl her anger against people or the pretty things surrounding her. The Chinese vase over there... that's it... yes, the vase... She would love to smash it in a million pieces.

The explosion inside her is tremendous; yet, outwardly, she appears in control. She is simply defeated and desperate, sapped of all strength; Martha has just made another discovery. If her Indian ancestry is such an obstacle to her integration in society, her social status would impede her all the more. In the taxi, on the way home to her mother, the terms Indian and Métis bounce around in her head. She feels nauseated: where is her place... if she has one?

Seeing Martha's distress, Gisèle cried:

"Good heavens! You're so pale! Are you sick?"

"Yes, sick about everything. I've had it with life!"

"You're only seventeen! How can you say such a thing? Come on, Martha, life is not always meaningless!"

Dry-eyed and frowning, the young girl's words cut deeply. Jacques Laperrière's insult was a lower blow than Claude Poitras'. Jacques had made her feel beneath the Mercure clan, but he was sober. He could have declined Ginette's invitation and finish the evening with her like a true gentleman.

The more she thought about it, the more she wondered how she could possibly have invited Jacques to her mother's. To offer him what? Coffee, wine? But in what glass or cup? Where would they sit? Facing her mother? In the one bedroom-come-kitchen-come-living-room? They would go inside and find an unmade bed and clothes all over the place. How humiliating! Her mother was tidy, but with so little space, just putting things away at bedtime was a challenge. Gisèle searched for the right words to quiet Martha's feelings in view of the blow she had just received. She had tried to give her a good education so she could rub elbows with Whites. But it wasn't enough to hide your ethnic origin when society attached so much importance to status, when what you do is more important than who you are.

After Martha fell asleep, Gisèle looked at her tenderly, searching her heart for a way to restore her daughter's confidence. Why not ask Philippe Beaudoin to organize a trip to Québec. Philippe spoke so often of his "belle province;" surely, he would be pleased to go with her and Martha. Gisèle's solution to sorrow was a geographical cure, to see new faces, change activities, make new plans. This was no time to think of money; Martha had to get away from the society that rejected her, to forget the affront of her so-called friends.

The following day, faced with Philippe Beaudoin's indifference, Gisèle insisted nonetheless, determined to give Martha a chance. Ever since her evening out with her classmates, her daughter had neither the strength to return to school, nor the courage to race strange customers from behind the counter at the National Bank.

"It's no place for a Métis girl," Martha repeated. "Better to leave the job for a White girl."

Bored and disillusioned, Martha loafed at her mother's, got up late and went to bed early. Classes were over, so she had no reason to meet her school friends—in any case, she didn't care—nor to see Sister Suzanne. She had agreed to teach music in the summer program, but she backed out at the last minute. In actual fact, she couldn't forget Claude's offensive behaviour, nor Jacques' insult; in spite of her efforts, she could not manage to put Robert totally out of her mind either.

Philippe's honesty was put in doubt when he began to come less frequently, and appear to be planning something.

Finally, a letter arrived from Québec. It contained magic words they read a hundred times over: *Come quickly, we're expecting you.* It was Gisèle's mother. No, her father had written it. Gisèle wasn't sure, and compared the precious sentence to the handwriting of two treasured letters. At first, fearing a cold welcome, Gisèle thought of visiting Philippe's family; later, she planned to phone her own family to seek a reconciliation.

But Philippe's dour attitude surprised her. He found a thousand and one reasons to delay the trip, finally refusing to accompany Gisèle and Martha: he would join them later. Disappointed, but determined not to let this wimp control her life, Gisèle suggested Martha leave alone as soon as possible; she would join her in Québec as soon as she obtained leave from the hospital. If Philippe changed his mind, too bad. She would drop him and go on her own.

"You'll meet your grandparents, your aunts, uncles, cousins. They'll be happy to see you, you'll see."

"Are they going to treat me like an uneducated Indian?"

"I can't make any promises. Ignorant thoughtless people are everywhere. In Québec you might find cousins as snobbish as in Manitoba; no one has a monopoly on this defect. Just don't let anyone take advantage of you. You're well educated and you have nice manners..."

"My father must have been so hurt to be treated like an outcast. In May, when I went to Atikokan with Diane Boucher, you should have seen what Whites did to the Indians who boarded the bus in Fort Francis. There was a woman who wouldn't let a ten-year-old boy sit beside her; the driver had to walk to the back of the bus to ask her to take her things off the seat so the boy could sit down. The poor little Indian boy didn't move a muscle the whole trip; he was just quiet and embarrassed next to the fat woman. Watching this, I thought of my father; the same thing must have happened to him at some time or other: begging for a place among White people. I wonder if Daddy is still alive... Do you think about him, sometimes, Mummy? Would you like to see him again?"

"I'm afraid."

"Of what?"

"Of finding him again, but sick and miserable. Sometimes I have second thoughts."

"What about?"

"Having married him. I never should have come to Manitoba. You know, it was a mistake for me to come here; but I made a second mistake by trying to make a White man out of him."

"But you want *me* to be White!"

"That's right, Martha, but you don't have a choice. You have to adapt to White society because, with your education, you'll never be an Indian. You can't even be content with being an ordinary Métis girl, because you're superior to many Whites."

Martha calmed down a little. Three days after her date with Jacques Laperrière, Robert phoned. She was taken by his voice and his laughter. She imagined herself in his arms, or sitting at his side. However, she resisted his tender words, and declined the invitation. Jacques' snub reminded her of Doris Gardner, another "uppity-up." She was too excited by the prospect of her Québec trip. she would have loved to tell the Lavallées and her friends she had relatives in the East... that she had been invited by her grandparents. Real Whites! This feeling of belonging enhanced her self-esteem.

Seeing the enthusiasm Martha displayed as she packed her bags, Gisèle was certain she had found a cure for her daughter's malaise; she was getting anxious herself.

"While you're waiting for me to get there, prepare my parents," the mother warned. "Here, take the two photo albums. There's a hundred little anecdotes you can weave with these souvenirs. Let your imagination flow; tell them about my life and yours. They know nothing about the West; they'll be interested. But be careful: try to keep quiet about my financial situation and my problems with Norman."

At the CN station, Gisèle hugged her daughter so tight when she kissed her goodbye, Martha was concerned:

"What's the matter?"

"What if we never saw one another again? Anything could happen... You might meet someone over there... Be careful, Martha, I have a strange feeling."

"Stop it!. No more gloom and doom."

In Saint-Boniface Philippe put in an appearance only on rare occasions; he seemed preoccupied. Whenever Gisèle approached the matter of the trip, he became sullen. One Saturday evening, they had just sat down to eat, when a knock at the door startled them; they got up at the same time. Two policemen entered confidently, asked a few questions and arrested Michel Desrosiers, alias Philippe Beaudoin, escaped from Parthenais prison where he had been serving a sentence for theft in a Credit Union near Montreal

Sixteen

On the train Martha enjoyed reading Gabrielle Roy's *La Montagne Secrète*, and occasionally engaged in conversation with other passengers in her coach or in the dining car. It was a lengthy voyage. Two days and one night listening to the monotonous or deafening sound of the locomotive. Only one thing mattered: keeping her mind occupied. She was determined to dump some excess baggage, to take whatever necessary measures to destroy all memory of Robert Lavallée, Claude Poitras and Jacques Laperrière. Above all, she needed to rekindle her own hopes for a better tomorrow.

It was no small matter: she remained haunted by the memory of Robert's burning kisses and passionate embraces. Yet she resolved to succeed in wiping away all trace of him and substituting happy adventures. She had destroyed every photo, every letter, hoping to block the path to her heart in order to overcome her sorrow. She would put someone else in his place. Maybe this nice soldier... near the window, who was staring at her...

If she was still bitter from her adventures with Jacques and Claude, she had also learned a lesson: to keep her place, to remain unidentifiable: no name no family. Had she stayed in Manitoba, she would have had to drag the ball and chain. In Québec, her future would be different.

As the train approached Montreal, the young traveller filled her head with new images and friendships. "I'll create a new world for myself," she thought as she grabbed her luggage with gusto.

In the waiting room, a couple stood apart, motionless, watching expectantly. Martha walked towards them.

"You look like your mother," they said in one voice.

The comment, revealing their refusal to admit the Indian features inherited from her father, upset Martha a little, but she passed it off, won over by their friendly welcome. He was not very tall, had a little pot belly, and smoked a fragrant cigar, showing a healthy mouth with a glint of gold; she was thin, taller, elegant and well-groomed.

The white Lincoln rolled along the freeway. The young traveller was fascinated by the scenery, so different from the Prairies; she had to concentrate hard to absorb it all and answer her grandparents' questions at the same time. Martha was delighted: there were so many huge trees; lawns came in every shade of green, and lovely flower beds scattered here and there adorned the well-kept properties.

Meanwhile, they drove towards the Bergevin's summer cottage, about thirty miles north of Trois-Rivières. They reiterated how anxious they were to meet their Western granddaughter. Martha felt they spoke from their hearts; she was definitely liking her "pépère" and her "mémère" who hugged her so warmly when she got off the train. She heard sniffling.

"Your mother's coming in two weeks, isn't she?" asked a sweet voice.

"And how about your father?" Monsieur Bergevin asked bluntly.

"Gisèle didn't say anything about him," Madame Bergevin interrupted. "How is he?"

Martha remained silent; however, she knew the two now regretted the past, how they had refused to accept their daughter's stubbornness. In their old age, they had become more understanding, and had forgiven the "exile."

The cottage was near the lake; white water lilies covering the surface suggested a Chinese pattern. On the east side, the second floor extended to form a kind of lookout. This would be Martha's room. From the window, she could see the cliff opposite, covered with an abundance of wild flowers and dark green moss, and shrubs she could not identify. Absorbed in her new surroundings, she didn't hear muffled footsteps coming up the stairs:

"Here, Martha, take this swimsuit. You'll have to bathe in the lake, there's no bathtub in the cottage. You can lounge in the sun until dinner time. Go on, it's 33 degrees out there."

"How did she know what I like?" she wondered. She detected a knowing look in her grandmother's eyes, and gave her a big hug.

"Thank you, Mémère. You're an angel."

She skipped to the end of the dock, raised her pudgy arms, threw them back, swung them sideways, up again, and plop! a splendid dive! Grandfather Bergevin looked up from his vegetable plot where he was busy getting greens for supper.

The cool clear water surrounded the traveller's tired body. She twisted and turned to relax her stiff muscles after so many hours sitting in the train. The smooth water inviting her to enjoy her new freedom, she turned her head left and right, diving again and again under the surface. Super! Life promised to be wonderful in Québec. They could swim earlier than in Manitoba. Robert used to say there are only two seasons in Manitoba, winter and July.

Martha would have loved to remain forever in the intoxicating sweetness of the crystal clear liquid, spotted with reflections and shimmering ripples. She swam to the water lilies, plucked five or six for the dinner table, and returned to cut a last one which she clenched between her teeth as she stretched out on the beach. Under a warm azure dome, Martha gratefully acknowledged a place of beauty and voluptuous pleasures; still swaying in the damp freshness, she experienced the full sensual caresses of the transparent element.

Eyes closed, and savouring each moment of relaxation, Martha reviewed her grandparents' affectionate gestures. Suddenly, she dived into the water again. One arm rising, then the other, she crawled slowly towards the cliff; swimming on her back she covered the distance twice over and returned to the cottage. She imagined her body floating away rapturously. When she opened her eyes, she saw ROBERT standing on the dock. It couldn't be! What was he doing here? She splashed through the water, her body stiffened, and she swam nervously.

The newcomer's resemblance to Robert was so striking, Martha all but lost her appetite sitting opposite him at table. The charming cousin, come out of nowhere, was stuffing himself with huge pieces of chicken breast, potatoes in their jackets, and garden strawberries and cream. He had only come to see the car his grandfather was giving him, and had to return to Montreal the next day. Watching him pour the wine, Martha believed him to be a man of the world. Curious about his personal life, she listened to every detail of the conversation, hoping to garner a clue regarding his marital status. The visitor let nothing slip by, nor did the grandparents, who seemed discretion incarnate. Martha was intrigued.

If he stayed longer at the cottage, Martha could swim or go canoeing with him, and satisfy her desire to flirt with the son of her uncle Jean-Paul's, the brother her mother spoke of most.

"Do you ride?" asked Pierre Bergevin. Annoyed, Martha had to admit she had never been near a horse.

"No problem," he added quickly. "It's normal for a city girl. Tonight, I'll give you your first lesson, if you want to come with me."

Surprised and delighted, Martha looked at Grandmother, who remained tight-lipped; Grandfather looked down at his plate. Were they reluctant to lend them the superb horses she had noticed in the hillside pasture on the west of the cottage?

"I don't know if..." Martha hesitated

"You can go," Grandfather replied gruffly.

While they were doing the dishes, Martha asked her grandmother why Grandfather had hesitated, and why he had got up at that moment to serve the coffee.

"We're afraid of accidents," Grandmother answered. "The road is narrow and bumpy since the construction of new cottages."

Riding behind Pierre, Martha was fearless. It was so easy to ride a gentle horse, just a little frisky, behind an experienced rider. After a short ride, they came back to the stable; Pierre mounted another horse, and left his cousin on Daisy, neighing her impatience to be off again.

Martha expected a short ride but when Pierre wanted to stop in a lovely spot covered with daisies and surrounded by birches, Martha was delighted. The charming cousin, the warm breeze blowing into the dusk at the end of a day so fine...

She told Pierre her bottom was aching, and she got a cramp in her left leg; she would have to walk around. She dismounted into her cousin's gentle embrace; he paused and placed her tenderly on a smooth slab of rock. He stretched out beside her, and, anxious to talk of anything other than riding, he blurted out:

"Would you like to visit Montreal?"

"With you?" Martha inquired.

"Of course, with me. Your first trip to Québec, you have to see the metropolis, see all the tourist attractions. If you could come middle of next week, it would be perfect. Pépère goes to town on Wednesday to pick up his mail; go in with him, take the bus to Montreal, and I'll meet you at the Berry-DeMontigny station. You won't be sorry, I can promise you that."

"Well..."

"Hey! Don't you trust me?" Pierre whispered, gently turning Martha over onto her back.

He leaned his sun-tanned face over hers, touching her lips ever so lightly; then he fell back, watching her reaction, before proceeding to seduce her. If Martha had been standing, her legs would had given way. How could she resist the charms of Adonis? Suddenly she threw her arms around his neck and kissed the mouth whose warmth recalled another. Her passionate embrace revealed the naiveté of a woman who has seen hurt and deceit. Was it Pierre's love she wanted, or was she trying to relive the emotions she had felt in Robert's arms?

They remained there a long time, kissing under the aspen and maples, a rare scene in this isolated forest grove. Gradually, all the breaks in the trees had turned dark; but Martha had only one wish: to go on forever trembling under her cousin's caresses. Was it a cure or a vengeance?

She couldn't describe what she felt, there in the arms of a man whose existence she didn't even suspect the day before; yet she thirsted for his bewitching words of love. Even as she welcomed his burning lips, Martha disapproved of her own behaviour. Was this puppy love, or a true love meant to grow? Was she getting caught at her own game? In such a strange situation, she saw a Martha who seemed like another self she dared not acknowledge.

Later at the cottage, Pierre poured himself a cold beer, chatted about their encounter with two fishermen at the point, the saddle they had to repair during the ride, the many new unique cottages. Martha couldn't get over his cool, and how clever he was at covering his lies; she looked at him sideways, and found him disgusting, in spite of his great body and handsome face. The grandparents were only half-listening to his unlikely tale.

Before getting into bed, Martha locked her door, for fear Pierre would venture into her room. A guy like Pierre was probably full of surprises. She didn't think she could resist him. At two o'clock, she still hadn't slept a wink; Pierre's come-on put rage in her heart, yet her body continued to savour the pleasure of his caresses. "Gigolo! Liar!" she repeated to herself, tossing and turning, and throwing the covers everywhere. The next day, as he got into his car, the cousin hugged her goodbye, whispering sensuously into her ear:

"I'll expect you Wednesday, little cousin."

But Martha did not answer. She turned swiftly and darted up the three front steps.

In the afternoon, Martha was comfortably seated in the living room with large French doors opening onto the calm sparkling lake, listening to her grandmother telling her Pierre's story: he had a family—two children and a wife waiting admission to a psychiatric ward. He had had many affairs with young students in his school over the last five years, with regrettable consequences for his family.

Martha thought her head would split, especially since her grandmother had guessed Pierre had flirted with her. Silently, she stared at the mirror-smooth lake, wishing she could rid herself of the shame she felt at being as silly as he was. As well, she was saddened by the fate of Pierre's wife. Tears in her eyes, she looked slowly around the room, and discovered the piano under an old embroidered felt tapestry.

Erect and proud, Martha got up, went to the silent instrument, and slowly and methodically lifted the coverlet. Bach, Chopin, Beethoven—music, her spiritual medicine helped to rid her soul of the remorse about to overcome her entire being. She played furiously, as if the notes could purify and cleanse. The piano trembled under the weight of the chords—her hands determined to seek, more than ever, truth, love and fulfilment.

The harder she played, the more she felt the weight lifting from her shoulders. She tried to understand. "Pierre is just a human being; I have no right to judge him. I'm not much better, playing his game the way I did."

Behind her, Grandfather Bergevin was sucking on his pipe; from time to time, he looked towards Grandmother, winking to show his admiration for his granddaughter's talent. Grandmother had put down her knitting. The piano had been silent for so long!

Suddenly, Martha stopped playing. A horrible thought had just entered her mind. What if? No, she was sure of it: she was just an Indian, and Pierre had invited her to Montreal for his own gratification.

Seventeen

In the summer, Robert worked at the newspaper; as well, he was doing historical research, and spent long hours at the Provincial Archives on Vaughan Street. His mother's fiftieth birthday was coming up on July 15th; she could now drive her own car and walked with a cane. Robert gladly accepted to organize the family celebrations: a cocktail party at home, with presentations of gifts, and then a meal at a restaurant—just Jérôme, Paulette, baby Nathalie, his mother, and himself.

Whenever he had a free moment, Robert dropped into the Portage Avenue jewelry shops looking for bargains. Since his father's death, he took it upon himself to remember birthdays, anniversaries, and special occasions. At every celebration, he recalled his father's words: "I swear before God and my fellowmen, if there was a second time, I would choose your mother all over again." The renewal of his marriage vows was a thoughtful reminder to his sons of their parents' deep commitment, their profound belief in traditional family values.

Robert had to give up the idea of a gift of jewelry, but found comfort in the thought that one day he would give her something truly beautiful. The eve of the event, still undecided and rather pressed for time, he went to the gift shop he had passed on his morning jog. On the way, he noticed a sign on the dilapidated Maple Leaf Gallery on the corner of Saint-Mary's and Horace. Due to the forthcoming demolition, the narrow windows were filled with paintings offered at forty per cent off.

Robert entered the dusty premises. Behind the counter, the little blond salesman, so delighted to see a customer, forgot to promote his merchandise. The potential buyer listened attentively to the explanations about oil painting, wood block printing, watercolours, and wash drawing. He discovered canvases by Indian artists: he had no idea this form of art even existed in Manitoba; he went from one canvas to the other, marvelling at the colours and mysterious subjects. Reds, blues, yellows, beside curved, straight, or broken lines. He was fascinated by the sober alliance of tones and lines on a huge white background, and enthralled by the creativity of the Manitoba Natives; Robert perceived a profound echo of the primitive and desperate cry of the artist.

His attention was drawn to a pen-and-ink drawing, in the midst of the blaze of colours; he went up for a closer look. It showed a dock surrounded by a parapet, a fishing vessel with tall masts, a rustic house in the distance under an almost cloudless sky. Robert was taken with this scene; it would surely remind his mother of their last trip to Northern Manitoba, one Sunday in June. That's the one, the ideal gift.

The print was numbered 23/100. He had hoped to buy an original, so he looked around a little while longer, but failed to find an equally evocative subject. "Who's the artist?" Robert wondered. *Norman Star.* Is this possible? The vendor believed Robert's reaction was related to the price tag. He had the bent-over look of someone waiting for a sale to pay himself a decent meal; he offered a reduction from the asking price of ninety-five dollars.

"I'll take this one," Robert declared. "I like the subject and the simplicity of the lines." He added: "Do you know the artist?"

"I do. His name is Norman Star. He sends me canvases through Luke Jones, a Main Street Indian. Star lives on Hecla Island. See the title? *Hecla Island Wharf.*"

"Hecla Island! Hecla Island!" Robert repeated as he left the gallery. A half hour later, he knocked at Gisèle Star's address only to learn she had left for Québec, to be with her daughter. Astonished and discomfited, Robert slowly went down the steps, got into his car and sat behind the wheel. He remained there, dumbfounded at the turn of events. Surely, Martha and Gisèle could have had the decency to drop in to say their goodbyes to his mother; he punched the dashboard and madly kicked the floor of the car. However, learning of Norman Star's whereabouts alleviated his disappointment. He slicked his hair back contentedly, turned on the ignition, and roared away.

That same evening he strolled aimlessly along the Red River in Lyndale Park. He alternately paused on a bench, avoiding other walkers, or ran like a madman, trying to make sense of the recent events. If he wrote Gisèle to tell her he had found Norman, would she return with or without Martha? Should he believe Jeanne, who had declared Martha had left Manitoba for good?

He spoke aloud: "That's one thing I can't stomach. She could have called me. I phoned her at least five times, but the lady always has an excuse. Why don't I just face the fact she'll never forgive me. Just the same, what I did wasn't a crime: bringing Doris home and expecting Martha to accept her was just stupid. Oh, women!"

Chomping at the bit, Robert was eager to find a solution and swing into action. What could he do without making another mistake? He had already started procedures to get a bursary for Martha to take grade twelve at the University of Winnipeg; maybe he could get things moving along.

Robert's announcement added a little spice to Lucille Lavallée's birthday celebration. Even though the two women had left town without a word, no one dared say the word "ingratitude." In the course of the evening, however, Jérôme' s wife made a negative comment.

"Let's not be too hasty in our judgements," Lucille interrupted. "If Gisèle suddenly went home after an absence of twenty years, she must have had a good reason. And she was right to take Martha with her."

"Just the same, Mother," Jérôme protested, in an attempt to support his wife's view, "Martha could have stayed with you after the attractive offers you made. She does need the money."

Robert cut in rather abruptly:

"Martha owes us nothing. On the contrary, we owe the Stars a lot, and this time, we have to help."

As he spoke up to defend Martha, Robert realized he had forgiven her bad manners. It was essential to get the Stars together again. Later would be soon enough to get the Stars and Lavallées back together. Although in front of his family, he appeared to defend Martha and her mother, inwardly he found it difficult to comprehend their behaviour. He wanted to forgive, but he had mixed feelings.

No sooner had Robert decided on a possible strategy, on thinking it over, it seemed uncertain and unproductive; solving this type of problem was a new experience for him. Who should he write to first? Gisèle or Martha? Who should he look up, Luke Jones, in Winnipeg, or Norman Star, on Hecla Island? He decided to find out the status of the bursary he had requested for Martha, soon after his mother had told him of her plans.

He made three visits to the Department of Education, only to come out of the office in a foul mood. But Robert was not one to give up easily; he went to see Inspector Stanners, a man who had often stood up in defence of French-Canadian causes. He pleaded Martha's case so doggedly and eloquently, that, five days later, a phone called confirmed a deal was in the bag.

He wrote a curt letter to an address obtained from a friend of Gisèle's.

July 27th

Dear Martha,

I have two bits of good news. First of all: your father is alive in Manitoba, and I know where. The second: I managed to get you a thousand-dollar student bursary. If you wish further information regarding your father or the bursary, write as soon as you can, as I will be away from Winnipeg from the 10th to the 20th of August.

Sincerely, your friend,
Robert

The hours and days dragged on as Robert waited for the mail or the phone to ring. One evening, after dinner, Robert rode his bike to Saint-Norbert. He wanted to be alone, to think about his mistake, the girl he would like to see again, and a decision he had to make regarding his mother. She was getting along well on her own, but Robert felt she was hiding from him whatever problems she was experiencing. In her last report, the therapist had recommended two weekly sessions of physical exercises so she could walk without a cane.

He pedalled energetically, a little too hard for his weight: a flat tire stopped him just as he was turning on to the main street of Saint-Norbert.

"Get in," cried a middle-aged woman form the cab of her truck. "I'll take you as far as the co-op if you help me unload my egg crates."

Robert called his mother from the co-operative, to inform her of the reason for his delay; she announced Martha had just phoned.

"What? Give me her number. I'll call her right away. Send Jérôme to get me. See you later."

"Just a minute, Robert. Listen to me. I've been praying for you and Martha to make up. But if Martha is reticent, try to understand. You're getting a chance to break the ice; don't blow it. Do your best; the most important thing is to go slowly. No accusations. Be kind. Speak to her gently. No woman is going to resist a quiet, gentle approach. Do you hear me?"

"Yes, I'll try. Praying will help. Take your rosary, and don't waste a minute. There's no time to lose. Heaven is a long way from Saint-Norbert."

Before dialling Martha's number, Robert got a good supply of coins from the counter. He was nervous, his mind in turmoil. How would he feel when he heard her voice at the other end of the line? He was hesitant. After all, she had left Manitoba without saying a word. And she had snubbed him for Jacques Laperrière at the graduation ball. And the secrecy surrounding her departure. Yes, Martha had made him pay Doris Gardner's visit; he didn't need any more punishment. And what was one to think of the fact that Jacques Laperrière was in Québec at the same time? Maybe together. It would have been better if Jeanne, a sure source of information about various friends, hadn't told him Martha had gone out with Jacques several times in May...

Good heavens! Was he in love with Martha? Why did he insist on her coming back to Manitoba? For his mother or for himself? What about the bursary? For Martha, or to tie her to him? Now that he knew Norman Star's hideout, didn't he have the best pretext of all to see Martha again? He might even take her to Hecla Island himself?

Indeed, Robert realized his mother's health was not his only motivation to see Martha again. Her voice was clear, rich, and warm. At the thought of meeting Martha at the Winnipeg airport, Robert felt a warm current slowly invading his body. Martha would return to live in his home, and the household would once again fill with life and cheer... just like before. Yes, if she could only forget Doris Gardner as completely as he had done, the frost between them would melt like butter in a frying pan. Before she would have to do anything, they would look after Norman Star; Robert would find him a job, or if necessary, a doctor who enjoyed a good reputation among the Indians. Robert talked on the phone about twenty minutes; when he hung up the receiver, he was smiling.

On July 31st, a white figure appeared, in the arrivals hall, on the first floor of the airport terminal. He had arrived a half-hour early, and spent the time pacing, and looking at his watch, attentive to every announcement on the public address system. When he caught sight of Martha, his heart skipped a beat. He stood motionless before her, full of joy, but not daring to move, afraid to make a faux pas. He thought of holding out his hand—the gesture would be so strange, so mechanical—rather he swept her into his arms. Their passionate kisses were proof the hurts on either side were truly forgiven.

Eighteen

"Martha, you'll have to learn to drive my car before my *chauffeur* leaves for Ottawa."

"You're spoiling me, Madame Lavallée."

"You'll be able to use it as often as you want... at least until it blows up. Robert is pretty rough with it."

"Robert..." Martha sighed as she put down her coffee cup.

"Were you sad, having to come back?"

"No way! Seeing my father again, a bursary to study at the University of Winnipeg, living here again. I owe you so much, and I know it... You're too generous, Madame Lavallée."

"Do you love Robert?"

"I'm not sure," Martha replied quickly. She hadn't counted on Lucille's insight.

Lucille, usually so discreet, regretted her question; still she knew, watching Robert and Martha in their half-serious tête-à-têtes, or laughing loudly on the verandah in the evening. There was one thing certain: the two young people were fond of one another, but Martha was still struggling with her feelings for Robert. Was she afraid to be hurt again? Was there another reason? Martha had admitted she wasn't sure she wanted to marry.

Martha had a temporary job in a restaurant on Kennedy Street; at home, whenever she had a moment, she gave Lucille her treatments in the big bathtub Robert had installed in the basement. The results were encouraging, and if the two women persevered, they would be successful.

Robert didn't go out very much, obliged as he was to save a good part of his salary to finish his master's degree in history. He and Martha played tennis, swam, jogged or rode their bikes; but mostly they worked all summer; they promised themselves they would spend two weeks at a ski resort at Christmas.

They had got in touch with the Hecla Island General Store for information about Norman Star. The lady had said to Martha, on the phone, that the artist was nowhere to be found. Terribly worried, Robert had gone to the Maple Leaf Gallery; from the owner Robert learned Star had gone North with two Indian friends. Jones had been invited to join the party, but had declined for health reasons.

"Sick!" the gallery owner repeated. "Jones is a first class alcoholic. He'd sell his mother for a flask of whisky. The last time he came here I didn't recognize him. A wreck of a human being. I advised Star to send me his canvases himself, instead of paying Jones to do it, but Star said it kept Jones busy to go around the little Winnipeg galleries. If Star knew how much Jones drinks, he might change his mind."

"What if I went to meet Jones to find out more about the two Indians?" Robert inquired. "He must know what his friends' plans are. If they go farther north, we may never find them."

"It won't work. The guy has flair; he'd warn Star someone is looking for him. What makes you think Star wants to see his family? Indians have a way of protecting one another, and discretion to put any secrecy expert to shame."

At nine o'clock in the morning, the following Sunday, Martha and Robert left for Hecla Island. It was the 6th of August.

"I'm nervous," Martha admitted. "I haven't seen him for almost ten months. I wonder if he'll mention my mother. How can he not ask about her when he sees me? What about you, Robert? Were you surprised about my mother's decision? You know I tried to convince her to come back with me to Winnipeg? I told her she couldn't abandon my father, that it was her duty. Nothing doing, she never gave in."

"Your mother was unselfish for so long, Martha; now she doesn't have the courage to submit to him. She's seen a door open for her to make a new beginning. Why should she come back to Manitoba against her will? When she chose your father "for better or for worse," she took a big risk, and she lost. She doesn't want to relive the years she spent here. Mission accomplished! Can you blame her for living her life as she sees fit? She's not the one who left your father..."

"The night before I left, we had a rather painful discussion."

"Both mother and daughter must have had solid arguments," laughed Robert. "I know them well. Let your parents have their own talk when they're ready. As for us..." He drew Martha to him, and kissed her forehead, her eyes, her lips...

Martha stopped the car at Winnipeg Beach. Holiday-makers stood around the restaurant. Inside customers sweltered in the heat. Near-nudity was the norm at 30 degrees and more. Even the most modest accepted extreme exposure, in a Manitoba where sunshine had been scarce since the beginning of summer. Buried under several layers of clothing for ten months of the year, the human body sought to satisfy its craving for sunshine and fresh air near the many lakes.

After their second stop at Arborg, Robert took the wheel. Martha had been driving for quite a while, and was showing signs of fatigue and stress. In Riverton, she insisted on stopping at the general store, a typical rural establishment stocking a million things from matches to lawn mowers. She liked to talk to the villagers, observing their features, and trying to guess if they were Slavic, Irish, Scottish or Métis, asking about their work or leisure activities, inquiring about their arrival in Manitoba.

This time, she was pleasantly surprised. Above the last row of shelves hung her father's sketches. She couldn't believe her eyes. A note on the cash register invited visitors to find out more about the Native artist.

"Of course I know him," replied the merchant. "He lives in the musicians' house on the Hecla road. He was here the day before yesterday to set up this display of wood-block prints. All new. Tourists buy them in the summertime when they come through to the Provincial Park."

Robert noticed Martha's reaction as she admired a small watercolour showing a woman—her mother—her hair blowing in the wind. He bought it instantly. Speechless with emotion, Martha slipped her arms under Robert's open shirt and snuggled up against his robust chest. She was profoundly distressed: in a few minutes she would stand facing the runaway, and she feared his reaction. Would he be pleased to have been found? Robert, feeling her torment, rocked her gently in his arms, eyes closed to better imagine the life Martha might have enjoyed, had she been born of a different father... a White man.

Nevertheless, Martha had been rather lucky: two religious orders had been there when she was in need. Savouring a few sweet moments in Robert's embrace, Martha forgot her father for an instant, and thought of her mother's joy, and her grandparents', when they learned the Redskin was a true artist, respected in his new milieu.

They drove on until they reached the village of Hecla. It was not the kingdom of Oz, but still a uniquely charming spot, with the calm majesty of Lake Winnipeg stretching along the narrow road. Many a Winnipegger would have paid a fortune to own a portion of this magnificent lake. Near the vast silvery water, they found the musicians' house, just as the Riverton store owner had described it. Martha started as she spotted the old building amid a profusion of flowers and the meagre foliage of very young trees. Behind the house, there was a long, narrow vegetable garden. A gardener looked up between the rows of corn, and removed his large straw hat. He shaded his eyes with his hand, in an attempt to identify the visitors.

"Wait for me here, so as not to embarrass him," Martha ordered.

Robert stopped, his hair whipped up by a gust of wind, and watched Martha run in the sunshine towards a silhouette whose arms opened wide and quickly wrapped themselves around the pastel pink dress. The man caressed her long black hair, then stood back to look at his daughter. He drew her to him again, enveloping her for all eternity. Robert observed them through his tears. The happiness they shared, the father and the daughter, he immortalized the moment in a photo, as they came towards him, arm in arm. The man and the girl shed tears of joy. Never before had his camera captured scenes so filled with emotion.

Norman had gained weight. He looked at his daughter's friend straight in the eye, and invited him into his home, where he lived alone, like a hermit; the lake in front, the prairie behind, sun and wind on all sides. Inside, the house was wretched but clean; there were canvases everywhere—on the walls of the bedroom, kitchen and studio, leaning on rough easels, spread out on the floor, or against the walls. There was an orderly array of oils, inks, brushes, and spatulas. On a plywood sheet resting on two wooden crates, the artist had placed photos of Gisèle and Martha. The models were surrounded by a large number of unfinished sketches.

Her father's obvious loyalty was a source of consternation for Martha. He was standing away, his head hung low. She suddenly turned to him, put her arms around him, and held him close, as never before. At that moment, she was sorry for past neglect, and especially for her unspoken betrayal. They remained silent for a moment. Norman was the first to speak:

"You see," he stammered, "I haven't forgotten you. When I did these sketches, I was thinking about you."

"Daddy, why did you leave?"

"I thought you would be happier without me; anyway, I just wanted to take off. I needed a quiet place in harmony with my need for wilderness; life in the White man's world is just too complicated. You know, Martha, I just couldn't stand it anymore, hearing people always boasting about the White man's ways, in front of gullible and innocent Natives like myself. Here in Hecla, I've found peace and freedom."

"It's so isolated here. Do you have friends at least? Do you go out?"

"Sure. I have good friends in Hecla. And I'm busy. I play the harmonium in church and I'm on the school board." Star stood up straight. "Occasionally, I go out with some other fishermen; fishing is allowed now, on Lake Winnipeg, since the month of June. We catch jack fish, pike, pickerel, suckers, turbot, and carp. You should see all the activity around the fishing boats in the morning. People come from all around, and we organize fishing trips."

While father and daughter chatted, Robert stood apart, looking the place over. He noticed newspapers and letters on the table; he wanted to learn more about this man who took his canvases to the Maple Leaf Gallery and the other Indian who had accompanied him in his flight.

"What do your two friends do—Courchesne and Jones?" Robert inquired.

"Courchesne works in Morton; he comes by once in a while. Jones... Jones... Well... He went back to Winnipeg; I just heard some bad news. He asked me and Courchesne to visit him in jail."

"So?" said Martha.

Norman sighed with satisfaction, a twinkle in his eye.

"Now that I've been found, I can go around Winnipeg without fear of getting arrested."

"You'll come to Winnipeg?"

"Next week, to see about Jones. Later in September, for a show at the Winnipeg Art Gallery."

"Hey!" Martha and Robert exclaimed in unison.

"Can we see the pieces you're preparing?" Robert ventured. He was fascinated by this individual, so different from what he had imagined.

Norman slowly put his hand through his shiny hair, shrugged, took a few steps, paused, then turned and went into his bedroom. He came back out, like an inquisitive child fearing a reprimand, and proffered a large oil painting. It showed a very young Martha, bright-eyed, with round dimpled cheeks and generous lips revealing sparkling white teeth. It was entitled: *A Métis Princess.*

They laughed and congratulated the artist. He said little. He was as modest about his artistic achievement as he had been about his musical talents long ago when Gisèle used to throw her arms around him. This time it was Martha hugging him warmly, nestling against his chest, savouring his odour of nature and fresh air. She whispered:

"Daddy, you're fantastic. I feel like I'm discovering a new man, seeing you here, surrounded by your paintings, musical instruments, fishing and hunting gear. And you seem so happy, so relaxed."

The man remained silent. He struggled to catch his breath, overcome with unspeakable joy.

Nineteen

On September 2nd, the crowd awaiting Norman Star's arrival at the Winnipeg Art Gallery is made up of an even number of Whites and Natives. The curator glances alternately at his watch and towards the double doors. Nervously, he explains one of the artists has a long trip to make, and that the ceremony will be delayed for a few minutes.

Martha whispers to Madame Lavallée: "I just hope Daddy will look neat. I don't want to be ashamed of him."

She's sorry now she didn't send him a pair of trousers and a jacket. When he returned from Hecla, Lucille had offered her deceased husband's clothes, but Martha had refused. At least she should have bought him new ones.

Suddenly, Martha is thunderstruck! There's Claude Poitras in the gallery with two strangers, probably fellow students in the Fine Arts faculty; he's given up Law.

"Calm down," Robert advises, squeezing her moist little hand.

Martha doesn't hear his comment, drowned out by the cheers of the crowd acknowledging Norman Star, arriving with the Sinclairs and a dozen young people. He is wearing dark trousers and a white turtle-neck sweater. He immediately joins the other artists at the podium.

During the ceremony, there is special praise for Norman Star's coloured canvases. Connoisseurs and novices alike, in awe of the complexity of the creative act, are fascinated by the flamboyant birds, their black streaks forming lines stressing the illusion of graceful flight. Gradually, little red stickers appear, indicating the paintings have been sold. For the first time in her life, Martha feels proud of her father, trying to imagine his feelings.

Lucille soon makes her selection: a small canvas showing a sun whose rays imitate ocean waves. *A Métis Princess* receives high praise. The director, William O'Connor, describes it as violent, warm, and provocative.

"Not for sale," O'Connor repeats. "You ask why? It goes without saying: just look around: the model is right here in this room."

Martha is unpleasantly surprised by Mr. O'Connor's remark. Just at that moment, Claude and his friends are studying the canvas with a lady, probably their university professor. Having determined to hide her Métis ancestry, Martha is now imagining the scorn coming from the boy who had been right to say she was a wild Indian. Upset and ashamed, she runs to the safety of the ladies' room.

She leans her head against the wall, hiding her face in her hands. She fights the panic surging inside her. A few tears of rage quiet her somewhat. She stands before the washroom vanity, examining her reflection in the mirror; to regain her composure, she throws her head and shoulders back proudly. Her red dress and silver earrings are becoming, but no amount of dressing-up or jewelry can erase the Métis features. She can admit to herself she was wrong in trying to make herself White; she knows she will have to face more disappointments, if she cannot accept her mixed blood, and take her truthful place in society.

"Tomorrow, everybody will read the *Winnipeg Free Press,* and know I'm Métis, and Norman Star's daughter." She brushes her hair vigorously; she wears it long now, like the lovely Doris Gardner.

Lucille opens the door slowly, and comes forward, leaning on her cane; she tells Martha that Robert is getting impatient, but to take her time and not to worry. Martha, once again recognizing Lucille's tact in trying to calm her nervousness, explains why Mr. O'Connor's comments upset her.

Meanwhile, Robert is pleased he delayed his return to Ottawa. From now on, Martha will have no reason to doubt the man who has found his true path, better than she could have done herself. He's especially happy to have been instrumental in the father and daughter's reconciliation.

At the back of the room, Norman Star is surrounded by his young admirers who made the trip from Hecla to take part in the celebrations—musicians from the orchestra he leads— and the Sinclairs, knowledgeable in Indian art, seeing Madame Sinclair's father also paints.

With two long strides, Robert is beside the guest of honour congratulating him and talking about the painting he covets. He must have this painting! The two men whisper back and forth, and Robert returns to his place, smiling with satisfaction.

When Martha returns to the gallery, her eyes look swollen under freshly applied make-up. Lucille, her legs no longer able to support her, is resting in an armchair a little apart from the gathering. Martha goes over to say she would like to leave as soon as possible. Robert exclaims:

"What's come over you? You should be pleased about what's happening to your father. Instead, you're disappointed and out of sorts. You want to leave? Can't you think what this day means to him? Can you imagine how he would feel if you left before lunch? Try a little, won't you?"

"Robert, if you only knew, you'd understand and see I'm right. I'd rather go elsewhere to explain."

"I've just invited your father to come to our house, while the Sinclairs tour the city with the young people. Wait a bit longer. Anyway, I spoke to your father about the painting... Well, what's the matter with you? You're not even listening."

In one breath, in an attempt to free herself of the feeling of asphyxiation, she spurts:

"I'm ashamed to be Métis. I've always tried to hide it, and today, this O'Connor had to proclaim I'm Norman Star's daughter. I've never felt so small in all my life... humiliated, really."

Robert placed his hands on Martha's shoulders, and stared at her, wondering if this was the moment. He stammered, and blinked as if holding back tears. Martha forgot her own distress, as she focused her attention on Robert's concern. Finally, mysteriously, half-serious, half-joking, he let out:

"I am also Métis."

"What are you saying?"

Twenty

The meal at the Lavallées' was festive, especially as Martha had immediately told her father of Robert's Amerindian ancestry. Who could had believed it? Robert had no Métis features. Lucille, intrigued by her son's confession, wondered where he had obtained his voluminous documents on the family. Where did he get his first clue about his Indian blood? In the past, her husband had insisted she cover up the matter; later, they had lied cleverly when Robert had had to do a paper on his genealogy. However, since Martha had come into their lives, Lucille had often wondered if there was any point in keeping this secret.

That evening, Robert felt he was burying his father's shame by revealing to his mother and their guests, the history of the Lavallée family; besides, he felt closer to Martha as he showed her the treasures from the portfolio he took out of his bedroom closet. When Robert had moved to the basement room, Lucille had noticed him carrying the precious file downstairs, but then dismissed it as normal caution on the part of a history student.

The first ancestor from Sainte-Anne-de-la Pocatière, in Québec, had served for three years with the Canadian Northwest Company around 1798. According to two letters in the National Archives in Ottawa, written by a Company factor, Jean-Baptiste Lavallée had worked hard as a paddler. Long days on the water, and nights sleeping on bare ground under the canoe, exhausted by portages, transporting canoes and cargo, soaked to the bone fording a river or crossing falls and rapids. Fearing for his life, Jean-Baptiste Lavallée had gone only as far as Fort William where he married an Indian named Cherry Raintree.

Later, his son Louis plied the route between Fort William and the Saskatchewan River.

As *hivernant*, he spent the winter in the various forts of the interior. On his return, he married an Indian woman, Lily Sunset, whom he took East to meet the Lavallée family. Unfortunately, according to the journals of a missionary priest, the Western Métis received a rather cold welcome. But the bon vivant overcame his humiliation, and amassed a fortune in the West, criss-crossing the country looking for furs. Having sworn to never again set foot in Québec, he concentrated his efforts on the fur trade. His attitude pleased the factors and Oblate missionaries, who appreciated the influence Louis Lavallée had on the Indians.

One of his sons, Napoléon, was in Saint-Boniface during the events of 1870, where he attended school with Louis Riel's younger brothers. As for his wife, Robert knew only she was called Mary, and she was not Native; her father had given her a farm and had tried to teach his son-in-law a few principles of agriculture. Unfortunately, Napoléon Lavallée had never been interested in "scratching the earth". A bon vivant of rather questionable reputation, he had several times smuggled stolen horses across the border from the United States. Shrewdly clever, Napoléon, following his wife's advice, had managed to have his three sons and five daughters educated in the colleges and convents of Red River. The youngest, Denis, had been one of the first to receive a Bachelor of Arts degree from the Saint-Boniface Jesuit College; he had even gone to study music in Toronto where he met Daisy McDermot, a Scottish woman who spoke excellent French and had such manners as to shame the province's best educated young ladies. The photo of her Robert produced triggered ohs and ahs around the table. It passed from hand to hand, while the historian answered questions about Denis, whose story he had heard from his parents.

Robert doubted his parents were totally ignorant about his great-grandparents, except, of course, the details about grandmother McDermot's education and grandfather's music studies. He was puzzled by one thing: which one of his parents had insisted on hiding the Lavallées' Indian ancestry?

Seeing his mother had never hesitated to take Martha into her home, and she had never objected to his dating the young Métis girl, he felt his father must have been responsible for this attitude; in any case, he was not about to blame either one in this matter. His grandfather had changed his name from Lavallée to McDermot to obtain employment with the CNR in Winnipeg; it appeared the Lavallées did not want Whites to look down on them.

"Mother, do you know why Daddy spoke English with Francophones?"

"Your grandfather did the same. The Lavallées were afraid to betray their Métis accent. In English it was harder to detect their ethnic origin, but in French, their accent was obvious in how they pronounced certain words."

"This chart with the names of the heads of families and their offspring is fascinating."

Martha was going through the documents spread out on the table. "I'd love to have one for my family. Would you help me make one, Robert?"

"Of course," Robert laughed, "as soon as I've filled all the empty spaces on this one, in two or three years time, I'll work on your genealogy."

"Where did you get your information, Robert?" Lucille asked for the second time. "And the time to do all this research?"

"In Ottawa, when I was homesick, I'd go to the Archives and poke around in genealogy books, parish registers, missionary journals, whatever file I came across. It made time fly."

Norman Star had listened to the conversation with interest tinged with sadness. That Indian women—perhaps his own tribe—had lost their identity by marrying White men reminded him of his childhood in Fort Alexander. He was certain Martha would never regret going over to the Whites. But, for him, this incursion in the Lavallée family history made him all the more eager to answer the call of his race.

The arrival of the Sinclairs put an end to the gathering, and they parted cheerfully. The Sinclairs, upon making Martha's acquaintance, invited her to visit. On Hecla Island, she could stay with them if Norman's house was lacking in amenities.

"I'd like to accept," Martha answered, giving Madame Sinclair a hug. "How can I ever thank you for your kindness to my father? You were so good to him," she whispered.

"You want to show your appreciation?" asked Mrs. Sinclair. "Just come to Hecla. We would be delighted and so would your father."

Winter, on Hecla Island, was long and terribly cold. To escape bouts of loneliness, Norman accepted the Sinclairs' invitation to teach him ice fishing. He had often heard of setting nets under fifty-inch thick ice.

"First, you cut a hole," ordered Sinclair.

"And then what?"

"Then? You cut another one a hundred yards further down."

When the two holes were cut, they set a jigger to float between the ice and water, attached a net to it, and left it there for at least a week.

Norman cheered at the sight of sixty or so pike and pickerel when he drew his net for the first time. That winter, he went fishing three times. For himself and his dog, fish was an excellent source of protein. Besides, the activity was a change from painting and brought in a bit of money.

On fishing days, one thing bothered him: his inability to have alcohol with the Métis who consumed large quantities of gin and whisky. While they slugged a couple behind their wool scarves, he looked away or took a walk to appease his desire to "warm up." He was so cold under his thin clothing; it was torture. How he missed the warm sweater Gisèle had knitted or a hot meal at the end of the day. He ate very little now.

Norman had a lot to learn about Indian tribes, especially his own, the Saulteux. If an Indian came to his door, he immediately invited him to stay the night; he took every opportunity to ask about his life style and his ancestors. Once he had given hospitality to a couple and the wife had made delicious pancakes covered with bacon slices and sprinkled with syrup; the dish reminded Norman of something similar his mother used to make.

He asked the visitor why Indians did nothing to regain their rights. Had they not had enough of being second-class Canadians?

"We're not Canadian," replied Billy proudly.

"Then why don't you do something?" Norman insisted. "Have you at least made progress after so many years?"

"No. We don't even agree amongst ourselves. And then hundreds of Indians have gone over to the Whites, women especially."

Norman hung his head. He was ashamed to realize he had never much cared about the Indian question. He had mostly sought his own happiness. If only Martha... but his daughter's problem was unlike his own. At that moment, a fit of coughing forced him to get up to take a few spoonfuls of cough medicine.

"If you saw a medicine man, he would cure your cough," advised Billy. He was concerned by the severity of the cough. "You're tearing your lungs out. Besides, you're going to die alone, with no one to lead you to the gods."

Twenty-One

Norman was perspiring although he walked slowly; at the post office he had picked up a letter addressed in a strange hand. Puzzled, he opened the envelope immediately. He was astonished to find the letter was signed by Robert Lavallée, who announced the discovery of a historical document of which he included a copy. Flattered by this honour, Norman walked home quickly; he sat down at the table to read through the letter signed by Louis Riel himself. Was this possible?

To Monsieur Pierre Lavallée
Clerk of the Court for Marquette-Est
Clerk and Treasurer of the Municipality of
St-François-Xavier

Dear Sir and Good Friend,

I am pleased to know the public has shown its confidence in you. I congratulate you. And I encourage you to do whatever is in your power to foster this confidence: I entreat you with all my heart to use your honourable position to promote the most cordial understanding between Métis and Canadians.

I would ask you remain friendly with the clergy. For, if you obey the clergy, if your compliance is enlightened and sincere, you are certain to please God; and you will be protected as we know you have been in the past.

When you see a Canadian show annoyance at the Métis way of life, you must try to appease him, if possible, by suggesting, if the Métis have many faults, they also have important qualities. Here is my own list of the fine qualities I see in our dear Métis countrymen. After the clergy, the Métis are superior to Canadians in the following ways:

1. their faith in God is truer and simpler
2. their Christian aspirations are more fervent and perfect
3. they are far more charitable and generous
4. they are more modest in their mode of dress and appearance
5. they are more honest in all their social exchanges
6. they show courtesy in a more natural and cordial manner
7. they curse, blaspheme or swear far less
8. they are peace-loving and gentler in all their relationships
9. they are more patient in any kind of difficulty or distress
10. they think and judge more equitably
11. their life is in harmony with nature, and thus less extravagant
12. they forgive insults more readily; they willingly excuse their fellow-man
13. they are more respectful and submissive
14. they are satisfied with less
15. they speak less
16. they are better judges of character and disposition

Physically, the Métis are better than Canadians in these ways:
1. They are stronger; 2. they are more resistant to disease and various deprivations; 3. their bodies are more energetic; 4. their eyesight is keener, clearer and stronger; 5. on the whole, they have a better physique; 6. their gait is steadier; 7. their faces show more kindness; 8. they enjoy better health. All things considered, let us first of all be Métis.

My dear friend, take great care to show the positive side of Métis character in such a manner that no one takes offence. Persuade Canadians the Métis love them. And instead of letting our people foster bitterness against our countrymen from Lower Canada, by overly stressing the faults of character these precious immigrants manifest, concentrate your efforts on showing the good qualities French-Canadians possess and praise the advantages they have over the Métis, some of which are very important. Proclaim openly :

1. French-Canadians are better educated
2. French-Canadians are more artistic
3. French-Canadians have more experience
4. French-Canadians work harder
5. French-Canadians are more constant
6. French-Canadians are more meticulous
7. French-Canadians are more temperate
8. French-Canadians are thriftier
9. French-Canadians are more disciplined
10. French-Canadians are more knowledgeable in many matters
Make a point, also, of reminding the Métis that, physically, the French-Canadians are 1.

lighter-skinned; 2. better dressed; 3. better housed; 4. capable of preparing better-tasting food; 5. richer.

Point out to French-Canadians what would be to their advantage to imitate in the Métis. And show the Métis how they can imitate the French-Canadians. It is imperative the Canadians and Métis cease their malicious criticism of one another's faults. The goodness of the Métis and the generosity of French-Canadians are meant to complement one another; thus the Métis can become more Canadian with the virtues of Canadians; and Canadians can become more Métis with the admirable virtues the Métis possess as a primitive people. It is necessary, let us be Métis-Canadians.

We must also take care to maintain in the minds of the Métis-Canadians a profound gratitude towards all who are good Frenchmen. For a large majority of our clergy is French. France has long spread its faith among us and the Indians, through its generous gifts. And today, in spite of the impious government which is causing so much harm, she continues to help the Church as much as she can all around the world. Let us be proud to be French. Our language, one of the most beautiful in the world, and certainly the most courteous, is the French language. Let us love the French.

Let us be Métis-Canadian-French.

Louis Riel.

Norman thought he was hearing the voice of the great Riel himself. He closed his eyes and tried to imagine him at the head of the provisional government at Red River. He vaguely remembered his history lessons, and the English publications that lent a different tone to Métis affirmations. This Pierre Lavallée who had received a letter from Louis Riel was probably an ancestor of Robert Lavallée. Robert's letter was certainly a sign he accepted his Métis blood and took pride in it. Martha's personality answered Riel's description, and Norman Star recognized in his daughter the traits particular to his race. After all, Métis blood was a mixture of Indian and White. By saying such nice things about the Métis, Louis Riel was bestowing a great honour on the Indians of Manitoba.

At that moment, a slip of paper fell from the folds of the letter. This time, Norman recognized Martha's handwriting. She wrote:

June 10th

Dear Daddy,
I will be in Hecla Island in a few days. My classes are over, and I want to rest a bit before starting work.

Your loving daughter,
Martha

Norman was a little upset by the news. He would have hoped to be in better health so Martha would stay with him instead of going to the Sinclairs'.

"What will she say when she sees me coughing my lungs out?" he wondered out loud.

He had correctly anticipated Martha's reaction. She found him in a pitiful state, wondering how his condition could have worsened so much since the previous September.

"Why don't you see a doctor?" Martha asked. "According to Mrs. Sinclair, there's a good one in Gimli."

"Is it worth the trouble for a little bronchitis or a cold I caught on the lake?"

"Were you dressed warmly?" Martha inquired.

"Probably not. Anyway, I haven't stop coughing since then."

"Daddy, let's start by going with the Sinclairs to see the doctor," Martha decided firmly. "Then, we'll take it from there."

Norman was too sick to argue. He accepted to go to the emergency at the White man's hospital. But he found the strength to oppose his daughter's decision.

"Never!" he protested. His vehemence had startled the nurse in the waiting room. "I'll never stay in the hospital."

Her father's desertion fresh in her mind, Martha was not about to impose her authority. She knew if he gave in, he would only desert a second time, and she would never see him again. Where would he go? With whom? Paul was not far away but would he leave his job in Camp Morton to go off again with a dying man?

"You'll catch my TB, Martha, you'd be better off... "

"First of all, you don't have TB. Rather a very bad cold and... and lung cancer. According to the doctor, you have only a month or two left."

No sooner had she announced the doctor's verdict, Martha knew she had been too brutal. She knew nothing about sick people... she observed her father closely. This man she knew so little was "her" father, the one she wanted to know and love during her stay on Hecla Island. She helped him get in the car, promising herself she would make his last days on earth as pleasant as possible. Like a gracious hostess who sees a guest to the door, she would be attentive and kind to her father to help him leave this world.

Mr. Sinclair tried to dissuade her from what seemed a senseless project, but Martha insisted, encouraged by Mrs. Sinclair's knowing glances. She didn't have to worry about Mr. Sinclair's arguments about being sensible, she had an ally!

"You can sleep at our house tonight, Martha," Mrs. Sinclair suggested. "Tomorrow, I'll lend you a bed, sheets and blankets, and you can occupy the little room where your father used to work."

"It's true," said Martha, "from now on, my father will spend most of his time in bed. But why did he wait so long to see a doctor? You didn't notice anything?" she added rather brusquely.

"Well... we thought it was mild bronchitis. Martha," Mrs. Sinclair added sweetly, "you have to let your father do what he wants. Don't just stay there waiting for death. Live each day to the fullest."

Once again, Martha felt gratitude towards this Mrs. Sinclair, a kind-hearted Métis woman who would be there whenever Martha needed her.

The first two weeks passed quickly, father and daughter enjoying being together. If anyone called to inquire about the patient's health, Martha encouraged them to stay as long as possible. She took advantage of their visit to run to the store or to the Sinclairs'. One day, the general store owner commented to Norman:

"I didn't know you had such a sweet and beautiful daughter."

Norman did not reply, but rather indicated he was not prepared to answer any questions. He whispered:

"Some other time, I'll tell you a bit about my life."

To ease Martha's financial worries, the residents of Hecla secretly agreed to buy Star's paintings. The majority were of delicate young women. Every face, every expression, every feature, suggested the spirit of Martha and Gisèle. No, Norman had not forgotten the two women in his life, his two princesses, as he repeated even now. If a painting disappeared, he became agitated. Out of consideration, everyone agreed not to separate him from his works.

Martha discovered the secret of her father's happiness on Hecla Island; he had found inside himself his dormant artistic talent, warmth and an inspiration he had been unable to express fully. One day, Billy the Indian came over and had a long talk with him. Martha overheard bits of conversation where they talked about burial on an Indian reserve.

The following day, Martha lingered at her father's bedside: she let him speak until he was exhausted.

"Martha, I've trusted White people too much, and Indians not enough. I wanted to get rid of my Indian face, and because I failed, I begrudged my people, hated life in the reserve and forgot my heritage. I denied my language, renounced my customs and traditions to adopt the White man's ways. I started to speak only English, sing American songs, and play American music. I didn't like French people before I met your mother. I even dreamed of a career in music in the White world. In the Fort Alexander Reserve, if I heard Indian music and songs, I covered my ears, because my people's heritage was synonymous with poverty and the lowest social status."

"Daddy, you must rest. You're talking too much."

"Before I go, I want to give you a message for your mother. Tell her I'm sorry I convinced her to come to Manitoba, and especially to have held her back when she wanted to leave."

"How did you ever convince her to stay?"

"It was easy. She was pregnant with you, and I said her parents would be hard on her, whereas I would..."

Martha was not listening. In her heart, the indifferent memory of her mother changed to pity. Her mother had been right not to look back. She turned tenderly towards the man who was once again humiliating himself as he spoke of his failure.

"What about your life in Hecla, Daddy?"

"The best days of my life. I want you to ask Father Dubois and Paul to look after me and bury me in Hecla, in a clearing near Lake Winnipeg. This way I hope to be forgiven by my race." Norman Star's voice was weakening: "When I'm gone, go to my father and mother in the Fort Alexander Reserve, and tell them what you know about me. Will you do this for me?"

"Of course, Daddy. I promise. I have only wonderful things to tell them. Now, just rest," Martha added with tears in her eyes. "We'll talk some more tomorrow. I, too, have a confession to make, but it's already nine o'clock. I'll get you a glass of warm milk, you'll take your sleeping pill, and get your rest."

Norman Star had confessed to his daughter the remorse gnawing at his soul. Three days later, Martha found him dead in his bed, seemingly at peace with himself, like a man saying goodbye to a friend he will see tomorrow. Martha was convinced he had gone to the gods to whom he would speak of his wife and daughter; she thanked "her own" Lord for his help during her father's final hours.

Twenty-Two

Two days before his death, in a moment of unusual serenity, Norman had talked at length to Billy; with Martha he had spoken of painting, music, and fishing. He had even inquired about Robert and *The Métis Princess* he had offered him as a token of gratitude for his kindness towards the two women in his life. He would have liked to live one more winter, especially if Martha accepted to be with him. In response to this wish, Martha had replied:

"I would like that, too. It would be so nice."

At midnight, he was sleeping peacefully, but Martha woke up with a start and rushed to his room. The next day, she explained: "He must have died at that very moment, and I was awakened by my subconscious." She congratulated herself on her optimistic reaction when he had expressed his wish to have her at his side. He had passed away so discreetly, sparing her the torment of watching him agonize and give his last breath. Afterwards, she whispered to him a hundred times over: "Thank you. Thank you, Daddy, for going so gently." Martha cried bitterly, astonished at her own distress; she had known it was coming, and had accepted it following the doctor's verdict. And she had prayed the Lord would take him, and not let him suffer. Only the strong blood lines between parents and their offspring could explain her pain at their separation.

Gisèle came from Québec, and left again the day after the funeral. Robert Lavallée and his mother were there to help Martha through these difficult times. In short, Robert had taken over the responsibility for the arrangements as soon as he received the call regarding Norman's death. After the funeral service, Robert wanted to take her back to Winnipeg;

they were well into August, and she had to register at the University of Winnipeg.

"Something inside me has changed," Martha replied. "Oh, I know it's not the road to Damascus, but I need time to think."

Robert took her in his arms, and reminded her of his trust and respect.

"Just as long as I'm still part of your life," he added. He kissed her tenderly on one eyelid, and then the other. "You need a rest, Martha. You're so pale. You said you needed a holiday, and then, you had the shock of your father's illness and death. Take it easy for a couple of weeks. I'll come back for you."

"No, don't. Wait until I call you."

"No. You can't stay here all that time. Anyway, you shouldn't be alone in this old house. The neighbours are too far away, and you don't have a phone. What if..."

"The Sinclairs are here."

"The Sinclairs? But you would have to go out to call for help. Listen, Martha. Come here during the day, if it's so important, but spend the night at the Sinclairs'. Promise?"

Martha did not reply. She reached up, and put her arms around him. He was being overprotective. She knew he loved her, and truly cared for her. At that moment, she was happy she had swallowed her pride and come back to Manitoba. Robert took her by the waist, lifted her up and spun her around before putting her down again. They kissed, promising to write regularly.

He kissed her passionately, unconcerned about Lucille observing the scene. She was waiting her turn to whisper her own best wishes. Martha would be missed.

As Robert got into his car, Martha said: "One more thing... Could you visit Luke Jones in Stony Mountain? Before he died, Daddy asked me to look after him a little. Don't be surprised to find him in a sorry state. A year of constant drinking, brawling and stealing right and left... and whatever else we don't know about... Anyway, he got seven years."

Martha had not told Robert of her long conversation with her father and Billy; she guessed he would oppose the plan she had concocted; when she had informed her mother of her intentions, Gisèle had broken down and thrown up her arms in despair; then, trying to soften her tone, she had censured the project:

"I'm so disappointed. After so much effort to make your life easier..."

She clearly disapproved of her daughter's plan to stray from the "pattern" set out for her. Her daughter refused to tread in the ruts that had left her mother with bitter memories; rather, she would venture on unknown paths, hidden from her for her own protection. She wanted to clear her mind of prejudices to make up her own mind. She had been taken in; and she would seek her own enlightenment. Following her father's example, she would consider Indians and Métis in a new light.

Robert was Métis but his features were those of a White man. Her own mixed blood never went unnoticed by those who knew the characteristics of her race: round face, chocolate complexion, childish smile, jet-black hair. If she married Robert, did it follow he would be proud to introduce her to his colleagues and their wives? She had been humiliated so many times when she was younger. "Once bitten, twice shy." She felt Billy's suggestion was her opportunity to kill two birds with one stone. First of all, she would discover if she had what it took to be a teacher, and secondly, she could analyze at length her feelings for Robert.

It was a little schoolhouse in a remote corner of Northern Manitoba, about fifty miles from Hecla; they needed a teacher for September; she couldn't get the thought out of her mind. In the last four years, seven young women had been at the helm, the last one leaving because she was pregnant. The "education authorities" at Black Bear Lake had requested a schoolmaster hoping for better discipline; their wish had fallen on deaf ears. In any case, as soon as an applicant heard the children were Métis and Native, that there were seven grades in one class, that the children frequently played hooky, and that the parents were more interested in boozing and sleeping around than in their kids' progress in school, he or she was never heard from again.

Martha had only grade twelve; given the precarious situation in Black Bear Lake, the Minister of Education had given permission to hire an uncertificated teacher. Sister Suzanne was pushing Martha to continue with her music; but Martha had given that up, knowing full well you need a roof over your head first.

Martha had never once considered being a teacher. But, no sooner in Hecla, they had begged her to teach the pupils her father had had to dismiss; along with piano lessons, she had offered help in mathematics or English. If she stayed, she only had to say the word and the town council would move the new piano they had just bought to the musicians' house. She could continue playing the harmonium at the church and direct the choir; there were twice as many members since she had taken over. She was driven by her desire to devote her time to new activities, to serve a community who would appreciate her new ideas.

Billy had promised to pick her up on Monday morning on Hecla Island, and drive her back on Friday, for as long as she was without a car. For Martha, it was an adventure in a friendly world, bordering on fantasyland. She had known only convents, city homes and streets; she couldn't get enough of all this space, the vastness of the land, and the big sky. She walked for hours on the lake shore or near the forest, enchanted by mysterious forces.

The sun had become her friend, the wind her confidant; she sought out nature to reflect and think out loud. At times, she stood in awe before the wonderful sunset and the sky arrayed in chosen fabrics and delicate hues.

Her huge dog followed faithfully, showing formidable fangs whenever a stranger approached her or the house, growling until Martha ordered it to be quiet. The dog Hecla had been terribly unhappy, three nights at a stretch without Martha; leaping and yelping, she had made it clear she could be trusted; she would prove it to them. The store owner explained a husky was too gentle and playful to be a good guard dog; so he trained Toulon to protect the young woman. The whole village wanted her to stay. So, with a telephone and two intelligent animals at her side, Martha had decided to live on her own without telling Robert.

Before his death, her father had encouraged her to paint. She did have some knowledge of technique, but she was grateful for his practical advice regarding choice of material, mixing of colours, and a step-by-step description of how to proceed with your first canvas. After supper, Hecla brought a brush, as had been her habit with Norman. Also part of the routine, the dog brought her slippers at sundown, and rested her white head on her mistress' feet.

Martha especially enjoyed the quiet cool summer evenings. She listened to music from a cassette player Robert had given her, she read, wrote, or painted. She was unable to explain her new fascination—totally ridiculous, according to her mother—for solitude; a newcomer to the island, she knew her attachment was temporary, and that soon the big city would call her back. In the meantime, Martha decorated the house with pretty wallpaper, painted the door and window frames, put up brightly-coloured curtains, and tried her hand at basic furniture.

There was an abundance of wild berries in the clearings and undergrowth, shrubs to trim near the house, and a row of lilac bushes Martha considered turning into an arbour. Whenever she stepped outside, she was immediately surrounded by the village urchins; they were eager to be of assistance, and the parents were delighted to comply with Mademoiselle Martha's every wish. The last Sunday in August, the young people assembled a cavalcade of eleven horses and organized a rather unusual parade: vans, horse-drawn carriages, cars, bicycles—even dogs—and a motorcycle toured the island. Martha rode a superb white horse recalling the Manitoba legend.

Robert and Martha wrote frequently and passionately. Their love grew. Feelings one did not dare speak about aloud were phrased with great sensitivity, and such sincerity as to confirm their faithfulness.

Things blew up, however, when Robert learned Martha had accepted the teaching position in Black Bear Lake, just when he was counting days till he could be with her again. He knew it was foolish to discuss it on the phone: he would have raised his voice and made Martha angry. He knew she didn't like anyone telling her what to do. He prudently decided to invite his mother to accompany him. Lucille hastily prepared the articles Martha had requested: winter clothes, music books, typewriter, books and school supplies; she added a long list of necessities a teacher would need to live alone five days a week and tend to dozens of needs.

As they neared the town of Gimli, Lucille spoke: "Robert, you're nervous and you haven't said a word about Martha. I know you well enough to guess you're upset." She paused a moment, then continued in a firm voice: "I suppose you can't accept her decision? You're getting ready to speak your mind? Things are heading for another break-up. Am I mistaken?"

"I don't want to talk about it, because I know what you're going to say," Robert replied.

"Okay," Lucille said simply.

"You're going to advise me to be gentle, to let her make up her own mind, to respect her decision, to think of herself and not me, and so on and so forth."

"Well! You're obviously a gifted mind-reader," his mother exclaimed.

Robert glanced at his passenger: she had turned down the visor to check her make-up in the small mirror. His mother's serenity was a source of wonder to him. Where did he get his temper and intolerance? From his Scottish ancestors? It was certainly not the Métis in him. They are rather easy-going.

"Let's stop here to eat," said Robert, as he slowed down to park the car in front of the hotel in the town square.

He knew what would come of his conversation with his mother; she was intelligent and thoughtful. The outcome would be positive; whenever he bounced ideas off her, it allowed him to think over various aspects of the problem, and avoid acting impetuously. In other words, to turn one's tongue seven times before speaking.

The last week in August, Martha rode in Billy's car, loaded down with suitcases and crates, on the bumpy dusty roads where they saw only an abandoned cart and the wreck of an old tractor. For a city girl like Martha, her first trip this far North was an exciting adventure. She didn't feel as brave as her idol, Gabrielle Roy, who had gone all the way to Waterhen: Black Bear Lake was not as far from civilization.

After dark, hundreds of insects landed on the Ford. They were strange beasts, about two inches long with motionless wings, as rigid as if they'd been starched. They were so numerous they coated the windshield: with visibility almost nil, the driver had to turn on the wipers and stop several times to clean off the mess. He grumbled:

"Such pests!"

"What are they?" asked Martha. She had never seen mosquitoes like these.

"We call them fish flies. They don't sting but I prefer mosquitoes. They don't make such a mess."

Gradually, Martha forgot about the fish flies, concentrating her attention on the new territory, trying to spot the schoolhouse of her dreams among the little shacks.

In the evening, she refused the hot gruel Billy's wife offered, and drank two cups of strong tea—she didn't usually drink tea—and listened to the report on the Black Bear Lake School. They showed her to her room behind the kitchen, and she retired to the little enclosure where she found a white metal bed, and a hand-made table and chair. A clothes-line stretched across the room. A chamber pot under the bed. No window. Whew!

She got under the covers, wondering what she was doing in this prison cell. She fluffed up her pillow, pushed her quilt off the bed, pulled it up again, tossed and turned nervously. She couldn't sleep, but why? She was tired enough after the trip in Billy's uncomfortable car on the bad roads. Her mind was occupied by a haunting vision, and a feeling she wasn't up to the mission she had chosen for herself. What she had witnessed that evening—yes, seen with her own eyes—was impossible to believe.

But it wasn't a dream. In the evening, Billy 's wife was baby-sitting the neighbour's three children: two of them were skinny twins with toothpick arms and hungry faces. When the mother came to get them, half-drunk, she handed the youngest a beer bottle filled with milk.

Twenty-Three

"Never! I'll never be able to teach, not even a minute, in such a dirty untidy classroom!"

With hindsight, recalling her angry outburst, Martha realized she had asked a lot of Black Bear Lake; on the other hand, she was convinced her attitude had been for their own good. For the first time, the parents had pooled their efforts to give their school an air of respectability.

Eyes wild, poor Billy had removed his John Deere cap and stared at her a while. He was disappointed. For one thing, she was overdressed for the occasion: high heels, white skirt, fine embroidered silk blouse, just to tell off the poor Métis people for the condition of their school. It was a classic example of an inexperienced school mistress. Seeing Billy wouldn't speak, she continued in the same vein:

"Why hasn't the place been cleaned? You knew school was opening in two days."

"Yes, but until the last minute," Billy ventured, "we didn't think we would get our own teacher."

She smiled, looked at the kind-hearted Indian, and in the hope he would forget her rudeness, she volunteered to organize the cleaning with a group of helpers.

A young Indian woman came to heat the water for the little urchins to clean the grime off their desks in the yard. When a child came to her, showing off a desk smelling of country soap, and asking to use it for himself, she signed him up at once. The mothers did the windows, walls and doors of the classroom. The room allocated for her living room, kitchen and bedroom was in a sorry state, but painting was out of the question. Fortunately, there was plenty of disinfectant, and it was applied freely to the corners of the closet to kill the vermin so Martha could put away her things. She was grateful to the jolly Métis woman who insisted on cleaning the teacherage first so Martha could get settled immediately. She surprised the parents with her announcement:

"Iss me gonna clean the shkool house now iss-a clean!"

When the hordes showed up on September 3rd, the teacher was aghast: forty-four children! Two pupils each in seventh and sixth grades, four in fifth grade, six in fourth grade, seven in third grade, ten in second grade, and the rest in first grade, meaning a total of fifteen beginners. It was quite a task for a girl with no teacher training. How would she teach the little ones to read and write? And when would she look after the older ones; who would supervise them?

They stared at her quietly, wondering how long she would last at Black Bear Lake... Some of the children were looking their best, even if it meant scraped and torn shoes, frayed trousers, or tousled hair. Nevertheless Martha found the kids charming and obedient. They responded well to kindness, and showed her affection whenever she came near. In spite of the relative success of the first day at Black Bear Lake School, she didn't sleep that night; she imagined herself aging ten years if she managed to last till June.

She expected good results with the first and second grades; the children marvelled at her lessons. At first, she found division three-four-five less interesting: the boys were lazy and a little silly, the girls lacked initiative and will-power. As for the two seniors, she had counted on them to tutor the young ones, but they proved to be the laziest bums, truants for the most part; trouble came soon enough.

It happened at the end of October: after recording a two-day absence, she contacted the truancy officer to register her suspicions. She was right. The two absentees were indeed at Sammy's, a bachelor of questionable reputation who attracted young boys to his house to drink and gamble whenever they had a bit of money. But far from stupid, Sammy refused to allow the police in without a search warrant. So the two delinquents returned to school at the end of the day, knowing Miss Martha would forget about their escapade.

For her part, Martha knew only too well sound educational principles required not to let this go, otherwise they would make fun of her, and do it again. Raymond had waited at the door, but Eddy, a giant at six feet, approached her, looking sheepish, to announce their return, but fear made her choose to react as if they had offended her personally:

"You can't come back here like this," she cried. "Not until I've spoken to your parents.

You can come back when they accompany you."

It was a mistake. It would have been better to accept them back, talk to them about the importance of attendance, impose a punishment, and pass it off as a normal childhood prank. However, the boys, in a panic, chose to take off. The parents inquired everywhere, but there was no sign of their passing. The children whispered among themselves, but Martha was unable to get anything out of them to help the parents track the boys down. Even the police abandoned the search, in spite of Martha's insistence.

The village merchant, fearing the two youths would break into his store for food, spent two cold nights guarding outside his establishment. Nothing indicated Eddy or Raymond were still in Black Bear Lake, nor if they had left. But he was nervous and worried, and ordered the police officer to find them or "to get the hell out of Black Bear Lake."

"Them guys have to eat. They's somewhere. Nawbody seen 'em take the bus. If I catch'em, I kill 'em," he yelled, punctuating his threats with curses.

The third day, a Thursday, the store owner's wife needed blankets for the household, and noticed the pile in the storeroom was diminished. Her warmest quilt had disappeared as well. She knew she had discovered the culprits' hideout, and ran to tell her husband; together they searched the furnace enclosure and found evidence of a hideout. They used the blankets to keep warm at night in the four-foot high space. Otherwise they were faring well. They had stuffed themselves with chocolate and peanuts—if the piles of wrappers were any indication—and digested easily with the help of pop and the store's best cigarettes.

If it hadn't been for the wife, the two thieves would have never left the hideout alive. Mr. Johnson was too angry to listen to the parents' entreaties, and even refused Eddy's offer to work in the store as compensation.

"I's never gonna have robbers in 'ere. Get the 'ell outta 'ere!"

The two "robbers" were sent to Portage-la-Prairie.

Eddy's internment made his mother angry; she was a flaccid woman whose resonant voice commanded a crowd. On her return from Hecla Island the following Monday, Martha listened to Billy; having already been threatened by the old shrew, he advised:

"Don't argue with her, Martha. Let her cackle. You won't be able to get a word in edgewise anyway. The worst that can happen is you'll get an earful."

It was a noisy encounter where Martha accepted every insult without protest; she noticed the woman's ragged clothes, sparse dirty hair, and straggly arms and legs. Around her neck she wore an amulet: a bear tooth to scare away evil spirits. She repeated twenty times over:

"You dunno hard times, you. I can tell."

Martha pitied her, and could not feel hurt by the undeserved insults; rather the emotional outburst commanded respect and compassion. The woman lived in constant fear of her husband who chased and beat her whenever he came home dead drunk. Hearing this last revelation, Martha got up and put her arms around the wretched woman's frail shoulders in a gesture of protection; her tears flowed freely, silently, powerless, with no trace of bitterness. The poor unfortunate soul calmed down.

"I'll look after Eddy," Martha said, nonetheless doubting the effectiveness of her promise.

Martha took a long time writing her first letter to Eddy; she couldn't sanction his misconduct, nor preach to him. What was done was done. Instead she spoke of turning over a new leaf, and attempted to interest him in new projects in Black Bear Lake.

The reply upset her. Eddy was happy in the Portage-la-Prairie detention home. He ate well, had his own bed, and clean clothes. There would be a hockey team, and he expected to be chosen as captain. His letter closed: "I'd like to stay here forever and never see Black Bear Lake again." As for school work, they found he was behind and had placed him in the sixth grade with Raymond; they were both starting to like reading. As for Miss Star, they didn't hold a grudge; as a matter of fact, they invited her to go and visit.

Delighted with the idea of going south, Martha proceeded to organize the trip with Laurent Sinclair's help. After they left Portage, she suggested a run into Winnipeg to cheer up the prisoners' mothers.

Her visits to Hecla Island were few and far between. As a matter of fact, since September she had gone only three times, because of the distance, but mainly because of the risks involved with Billy's old jalopy. School kept her busy; she couldn't afford to be off on weekends, if she wanted to be adequately prepared for Monday. The Sinclairs missed her, and from time to time, they went to Black Bear Lake to offer their help.

After Raymond and Eddy's arrest, Sammy, hoping to get even with Martha, knocked on her bedroom window one night. Toulon was at the door like a shot; he would have devoured the enemy in one bite. Martha immediately opened the window so the assailant would hear the huge German shepherd's fierce growling; just as quickly, Sammy took off across the yard, and leaped into the getaway car to join companions of questionable reputation.

The next day, the police informed the public that Martha was armed, and had permission to fire at anyone who attempted to frighten her. But the incident had upset Martha to the point she was seriously considering abandoning her post. In Billy's opinion, she needn't worry: the residents of Black Bear Lake knew of Sammy's aggression, and were keeping a close eye on him; if he dared annoy her again, they would look after him.

Martha continued in her job which she now regarded as missionary work. She pitied the numerous children who suffered from anemia; she saw them loving music, singing, and painting. The most memorable evening she spent at Black Bear Lake was the night when the Sinclairs arrived unexpectedly, bringing in their truck the old piano from the musicians' house. The next day, she played the piano, and sang with her class for the greater part of the day.

"We have to celebrate," she told the children. "We're not wasting our time. In Winnipeg schools, children learn music and singing; you too have the right to listen to music and learn to sing."

"Let's have a Christmas concert!" suggested tiny Tom, timidly. He had lost an arm in a hunting accident, and his large ears listened to music religiously.

"It's too late for this year, Tom, but next year, I promise."

"Will you be here next year?" asked Guy Vivier. "Here, we have a new teacher every year."

"Well, why not?" Progress was slow, but it was coming. And the children were so eager to learn, so hungry for attention and kindness. Martha loved them. She loved them ALL.

In Black Bear Lake, they jabbered in a mixture of English, French, and Cree; just the same they managed to understand each other. As Martha had only a temporary permit, an inspector from the Ministry of Education made three visits before Christmas. According to the first report, the previous year's chaos had given way to a strict timetable she kept too scrupulously.

The inspector sat in the desk vacated by big Eddy, and took notes as he observed her teaching. She was giving a social studies lesson followed by an exercise where the group found lakes and rivers on the map; then she went on with a science lesson for grades three and four.

The children knew time doesn't come by twice, so they listened attentively so as not to miss any part of the explanation; but more likely these woods children were fascinated by the life of rodents. Meanwhile, the beginner group practiced forming large a's, d's, and t's; From time to time, they sucked on their pencils, glanced at their neighbour's copybook to check if he or she was doing better, and to Martha's surprise, a few even went to Mr. Lalore to show him their work. He was obviously charmed by their simplicity and courage.

Around noon, as he left the little Black Bear Lake School, the inspector bowed and said:

"My hat off to you, Miss Star. You are doing a hundred times better than some of our diploma teachers. Today, I've seen a miracle."

She would have given him a hug if it hadn't been for the huge pile of books he had offered her, and that she held against her like a little girl afraid someone will steal her ice-cream. The man, seeing the excitement in her innocent face, stroked her cheek with the back of his hand, saying:

"You're a brave girl! Keep on. Faites-les chanter en français."

So Mr. Lalore had seen the sheet music on her desk. His effort to speak French to her— he enunciated carefully—was a sign he approved of her initiative. Anyway, she didn't just sing in French; at recess she spoke French to those of French ancestry, and she did a little oral practice in class.

On the fourth visit, she prepared simple words of thanks to the representative of the Ministry Department of Education for his encouragement and the confidence he showed in her work; he, in turn, advised her not to give up, as she was exceptionally talented, especially in class preparation.

No sooner had he left, Martha announced a celebration. They pushed the desks aside and put on an impromptu Christmas concert: Scottish and Irish dances, square dancing they had learned with her. Then she invited her audience to form a circle around the Christmas tree and she sat at the piano. Under the tree the children had placed their own dolls to represent the figures of the crèche. She wanted to make sure she offended no one, so all the dolls, wrecked or almost new, had been accepted. The school janitor was delighted to «play with dolls» for many hours, using the fabric scraps Madame Lavallée had sent. Her dear friend had added several yards of white and blue tulle to give the crèche a modern appearance, a style the children had never seen, even in books. The parcel also contained two new dolls, about eighteen inches in height; they could stand on their own and open and close their eyes; with their new silver wings, they would be the angels.

Fascinated by the tinsel and lights, the little ones came to school earlier than usual; they stood in front of the crèche, staring at the dolls magically transformed into the Baby Jesus,

Mary, Joseph, shepherds and Magi.

It was December 22nd, and sitting on the floor Indian style, the children smiled with joy—the only joy they would have this Christmas. Martha found them beautiful and calm. These Indian and Métis children had fine voices, especially the MacFarlane twins singing the solos that afternoon.

Robert was expected at any moment, and Martha had set the scene meant to prove to him she had been right to put off her attendance at university. She wanted him to say, as Mr. Lalore had done, that she was a brave girl; she also wanted him to speak to the children, to love them, to hear them sing *Adeste Fideles, Sainte Nuit, Petit Noël, The Little Drummer Boy*. Robert loved children; he would find them adorable. He would see for himself that by preparing the song sheets he had done his part in making a few people happy in this remote corner of Manitoba.

Her fingers ran on the piano keys, her voice blended with the children's in song, but her eyes were riveted on the window, watching the arrival of 'the car from Winnipeg.' She saw him turn the corner and stop in front of the teacherage; she guessed he wanted to see her alone. Great idea! She was just as anxious to spend a few moments with him alone. She whistled for Hecla who jumped in the fray, the children petting her and talking to her. Anytime she wanted to reward the children, she only had to let Hecla in unexpectedly—a cause for instant celebration!

"Ten minutes' recess!" she announced. "If you behave, there will be candies afterwards."

Never had Martha been so happy to snuggle in her lover's arms, to beg him to hold her close, to kiss him warmly and say sincerely and passionately:

"My darling! I've missed you so much!"

Twenty-Four

While Robert locked up the modest schoolhouse, a cheerful group accompanied Martha to the car. The older ones carried her baggage and gifts with the care of professional movers. The most extroverted, Paul Sansregret, signalled to Martha to bend over, plunked a kiss on her cheek, and ran to the back of the line screaming "Joyeux Noël!" He was so cute! John Sauvé, a third grade student, came forward to ask:

"Miss, what about the flag? Who's going to look after it if I don't come to school?"

Jerry, whose little brother was wasting away in a malodorous room, whispered in her ear:

"Pray to Baby Jesus to make Andrew better."

Little hands gripped the teacher's parka in an attempt to hold her back. She understood their bold gestures, hearing a little girl mumble:

"We're afraid not to see you again."

She was moved to tears, hugging the silent pupils whose supplicating looks tore her to pieces. They loved school: at home, it was cold, there was no crèche, no Christmas tree.

"But how did these poor children get the money to buy you gifts?" Robert asked, as Martha waved goodbye to a second group waiting like soldiers by the roadside.

"Well when I saw Billy's kids and the grocer's kids place gift-wrapped packages under the tree, I had an idea. Shyly, the other children came to whisper in my ear that they were going to give me something. Some admitted they had nothing, but if they had money, they would give me a "big, big" present. I had to invent some kind of ruse because it broke my heart to see how they looked at the presents with my name on it. So, I had this brain wave!"

Martha put her hand on the driver's wrist and went on:

"Don't laugh, Robert, but this is really funny. I plotted this with the janitor lady; I suggested she plan the surprise with whoever was willing to go along. She asked them to keep a secret, and bought and wrapped presents, making each one believe he was the only one. I paid for my own presents." Martha was laughing hysterically. "Would you believe it? The list of suggestions they made to Madame Vandal contained only useful articles; so I've received a toothbrush, a tube of toothpaste, a comb, soap, a pen, and so on. The older kids gave things normally bought by the school board. You know, Robert, Christmas is really painful for poor people who would like to give presents according to the custom; their hearts are just as generous as those of the rich. They're every bit as loving, but they can't show it without money."

Robert laughed at her ingenuity, thinking she would make a great politician. He replied:

"You're right. It must be cruel to have a heart filled with love and have no concrete way of showing it. Because loving is really trying to make the other person happy, isn't it? So you think of giving, even if it means depriving yourself... Miss Martha, I have a present for you, too, and it wasn't Madame Vandal's idea. You have to guess. Three chances, three questions."

"Will I be able to bring it back to Black Bear Lake?"

"If you wish."

"Is it for me?"

"If you wish."

"Is it for the children?"

"If you wish."

"Okay. Is it an encyclopedia?"

"No."

"A wall map?"

"No."

"A record player?"

"No."

"Okay, I give up. I can wait till Christmas Eve. Anyway, I love you," she added, tickling his neck.

Robert stopped the car at once and kissed her, confessing he had been extremely worried about her. The sun was warm, the road isolated, the moment perfect for tender revelations. Manitoba had never been so splendid in December, nor the lover's heart so earnest.

Lucille was waiting for them. The house was tastefully decorated. Martha stood in the doorway, in raptures. She was so happy to be back in Saint-Boniface! This felt like home. She had been lonely in Black Bear Lake, and had cried on many an evening, overwhelmed by the thankless task.

"The house is so beautiful" she said finally. "I'm so happy to be here in your home."

Lucille embraced her and whispered:

"I am as happy as Robert to see you again. Martha, this is your home. I want you to feel at home here."

Between December 23rd and 31st, the school teacher spent her holidays shopping, learning how to prepare favourite dishes, typed a brief Robert would deliver at a convention in Regina, attended two plays, saw a performance of the Grands Ballets Canadiens, on top of the many family gatherings at the Lavallées', and snowshoe excursions in Bird's Hill Park. She wanted to see this magical place again and relive the memories of her first dates with Robert.

Martha received a long letter from her mother: Gisèle asked to be forgiven for returning to Québec so soon after Norman's funeral, expressed her discontent at Martha's decision to teach among the Métis, and asked Martha to understand her reluctance to return to Manitoba. "Martha, you just don't know how much you are in my thoughts," she wrote.

Thanks to her parents' influence and financial assistance, Gisèle had moved into a cozy apartment, and had a job as clerk in a ladies' dress shop in Trois-Rivières. Bilingual clerks were few and far between, so Gisèle found employment immediately. Her brothers and sisters ignored her; their lives were miles apart, and they had become strangers. Nevertheless, Gisèle got along famously with her parents, in spite of their sadness about their other children's ostracism.

There was a second letter for Lucille; it contained anecdotes about life in Québec, and an invitation to visit.

"You'd like Québec, Mother," said Robert. "The Québécois know how to enjoy life. Taxi drivers, bus drivers, talk to their passengers; waiters and waitresses in public places are very friendly. They never stop talking, and roar with laughter. It's never boring."

Among her many activities during the holidays, a crucial one was a tour of the Salvation Army centres. Martha found skates for her fourth and fifth grade students, sweaters, tuques, and mittens for the grade twos and threes, and lovely little fur-lined boots for the smaller kids; their rubber boots were just too cold in 40 below zero weather.

The pleasure of bundling up her treasures for Black Bear Lake was for her a unique experience.

"If you mail your parcels right away, the janitor will be able to put them under the Christmas tree before your arrival," Robert suggested.

Lucille took the opportunity to also send items for the grown-ups: clothes that had belonged to her deceased husband, gloves, scarves, hand-me-down shoes and jerseys from Robert and Jérôme, skirts and coats she no longer wore. Trusting her treasure trove would bring joy to Black Bear Lake, Martha was eager to return to fulfill her promise. She had indeed told her pupils their gifts would come from Winnipeg.

The young woman made no effort to look up old friends in Saint-Boniface. As she reviewed her stay in Hecla Island and Black Bear Lake, she realized she had been privileged to know her father better, and to be concerned about giving the deprived young people of Black Bear Lake, her youthful energy, talents and, above all, affection.

She found time to go around the bookstores to add to her collection of history books and records. Sister Suzanne lent her music books for teaching rudiments of singing and music, and children's theatre; she gave her stars and stickers to decorate the assignments of the most diligent children. In short, whenever Robert left for his office at the University, she was busy preparing the second semester of school.

Robert insisted on playing Santa Claus with gifts of sweets for the kids, but he asked Martha to tell them who it came from. Was he trying to find a place for himself in their hearts? At the last minute he had included a parcel containing thirty or so games he had found in Eaton's basement at the Boxing Day Sale.

On New Year's Eve, in an intimate moment with Robert, Martha alluded to the joy that would come to those who were taking a more important place in her life. Robert avoided all reference to her second year at the school. Martha felt he was reluctant to bring up the subject for fear of casting a grey cloud over their holiday, and snuff out their happiness. She spoke constantly of "her" school and "her" pupils; but he was such an attentive listener that she spoke openly of her significant moments as a teacher, hoping, no doubt, to win him over to her cause. At one time, she thought he had accepted without misgivings her stay in Black Bear Lake, and even her return the following year.

"You know," she said, intending to put an end to her chatting to let him speak, "I really liked your text on the colonization of the West, especially the pages on the granting of land to the Métis."

"What did you think of the extracts from Louis Riel's letter on the characteristics of French Canadians and Métis? Do you think it will be of interest to the audience at the convention?"

"Your observations are serious and I learned a lot. I feel, though, that you don't understand the difficulties I've experienced because I'm Métis. How did you feel when you found out you were of mixed blood?"

"Well, discovering my roots sort of gave me new energy." Robert put his hand over hers, and drew it closer to the lamp: "I must make a decision, and I need to know your plans first."

Suddenly, the lights of the restaurant went out: the momentary short-circuit allowed Martha to hide her emotion. She was gripped with fear: Robert was going back to Ottawa and was seeing Doris Gardner, or else he was flying to Paris, attracted by Paris libraries. Was he planning to start his doctoral studies? Caught in between, she hoped she would be able to make a choice. Which one, though? Would she marry and go with him, or remain faithful to him in Winnipeg? Unless he was giving her her freedom as did many lovers before a final commitment? Since Christmas, she was certain of her feelings towards Robert Lavallée. Yes, she loved him more than ever. Besides, she had chosen to isolate herself in the North to test her attachment. And the separation had been painful; she thought about him, dreamed...

The thought of marriage was rather daunting, so she tried to push it out of her mind, like the idea of adultery or an unkind deed. Unable to either accept or refuse, Martha silently placed her left hand on Robert's. She paused. Robert was waiting for her to speak. HER PLANS? The moment had come, she would have to say something, but how? During this holiday, they had spoken so often of their love, they had to think of the future.

When the lights came on again, applause broke out in the restaurant. In the dark Robert had placed his other hand over Martha's; as they released their hands now, the lovers experienced a strange sensation of having been prisoner of the other for an instant. The silence became uncomfortable; who would speak first? Robert seemed determined not to start. Martha met his gaze, trying to read his mind. She admired his intellect. Could he read her mind? Did he know the dilemma she faced? If he did, then he knew she loved him passionately, and understood her hesitation. She wasn't ready for marriage. Robert decided to break the silence, and take her out of her misery.

"Martha, I don't need an answer before the end of March. In three months' time, can you decide if you intend to return to Black Bear Lake, or if you will register in University in September?"

Martha was relieved! Dear Robert, he again showed his respect for her by giving her breathing space. Finally, she spoke:

"On Saint Valentine's Day, the feast of love, you'll have my answer, I promise."

Robert presented her with a small case containing a gold pendant. At Christmas, he had given her a television set to make life more pleasant in her Black Bear Lake "castle" and provide entertainment for her pupils; but at New Year's, he wanted the gift to be exclusively hers.

The next day, Martha visited Jones. He spoke of Norman, the musicians' house he should never have left, and his friends in Hecla Island. In winter, he appreciated the comforts of prison, but had hated spring and summer between humid walls and asphalt courtyards: no sun, no wind, far from rivers and forested wilderness. His health was poor now, so he would never be able to fulfill his dream of freedom. For a moment, Martha thought of bringing him back to Hecla Island after his release from jail... that's what Norman Star would have done... poor Jones! He was more dead than alive, his prison uniform hanging loosely on his meagre frame. Martha said goodbye, promising to write; she thought of her father, and prayed to him to protect his wretched friend.

January in Black Bear Lake brought enough cold weather to flood a skating rink, and enough sunshine for Martha to extend recess time outdoors.

When the missionary visited, Martha offered him a cup of coffee, hoping to speak at length with this warm individual she felt she could trust.

"I must decide as soon as possible," she confided; "the school trustees have to hire a replacement if I leave, or request an extension of my permit. I don't have a certificate, you know."

"But you can't leave," exclaimed the big man; he sported a thick beard and bushy eyebrows. "What will we do without you? The school is going to return to the turmoil it knew before your arrival: wild brawls, mud shovelled into the schoolhouse. We've seen it all here, Miss. You can't leave. Things are going so well. Come now, be brave! Stay at least another year. Until the Sinclair girl finishes her course; now that the school is in better shape... she might agree to take your place."

The priest was surprised when Martha insisted:

"But, Father, I have a boyfriend in Winnipeg."

"A boyfriend... well... you want to get married? He can't wait a while? You're too young, anyway. How old are you?"

"Nineteen."

"Nineteen? You Métis, you get married too young. What's the rush? What does he do, your boyfriend?"

Martha was silent, and the missionary repeated:

"What's his job?"

"He's a professor of history at the University of Winnipeg."

"Oh, well! But that doesn't change my advice. Do like the French. Put a damper on this. Take your time. Finish your studies, take advantage of your youth, and prepare to take your responsibilities when you're more mature."

In the evening, Martha phoned Robert and told him of her conversation with Father Bourquier. Before hearing her out, he asked nervously:

"You're staying?"

"Yes," she replied abruptly, determined to have it out and forget the consequences of her decision.

"Martha, your decision is going to work out okay."

"I don't understand."

"Are you coming to the Festival du Voyageur with your students?"

"Yes, Laurent Sinclair agreed to drive the bus, and Billy is coming along in case we have problems. A trip like that is risky with children at this time of the year. It's been bitterly cold in Hecla for the last two weeks."

"Okay, I'll expect you next week and we'll talk about your decision and mine."

Martha was unsure if the atmosphere was full of promise or grief. She was already sorry she had sacrificed Robert's wishes for her own altruistic inclinations.

Twenty-Five

As she prepared for the student trip, the young teacher was preoccupied as much with the thousand and one details of the adventure as by the reasons she would give Robert and the possible outcome of their conversation. Would her determination to teach in Hecla for two years cost her dearly? Was a break-up inevitable?

In Hecla, the kids were excited. They had never been to Winnipeg. The tourist pamphlets and brochures Robert had sent were dog-eared and faded, victims of so much handling and detailed scrutiny.

Laurent Sinclair proved to be an excellent driver, and Billy was dedicated to his passengers' every need. At the end of the day, the Indian was as happy as Martha when the bus stopped in front of Précieux-Sang School where the principal awaited the arrival of the forty youngsters. He took them to the gymnasium where ladies gave each child a substantial snack and a sleeping bag. It had been agreed Martha would spend the three nights at the Lavallées'; she didn't have to worry, the two supervising adults would get the children up in the morning, and to bed at night.

She was just finishing her last recommendations, when she felt a warm presence behind her, and two hands blindfolding her. He was there. It was a good sign. A few words to Billy... and the couple left the school hurriedly in the car waiting for them in front of the school.

Lucille had left a note on the hall table: "Back in a few minutes."

"Always so tactful," observed Martha. She could say no more. Robert swept her into his arms and kissed her passionately.

Immediately their conversation turned to serious matters: Martha's intentions, Robert's plans, Madame Lavallée's future.

"Do you understand? I've been offered a position in the Department of Native Studies at the University of Brandon; I can't accept until I know your own plans. Martha, if you start your program in education in Winnipeg, that means we'll be apart for at least four years. On the other hand, if you teach a second year in Hecla, you'll be satisfied and go into teaching with greater assurance. Teaching is such a demanding profession. As for me, I'll find out if I like the job or not."

"And then what?" Martha asked, rather puzzled.

"Well, then, after that..." Robert was obviously pleased Martha had taken time to think things over. "You can come and join me in Brandon and register at the Faculty of Education there."

"You're not going to do your doctorate in history?"

"Sure, but later. While I'm teaching, I can start on it... But, Martha, let's talk less about studying and more about us." Serious now, he whispered in her ear: "Together life will be beautiful; I'm love-sick over you, and I'll never recover..."

"Robert, you're a part of my life now forever. I was so afraid of what you would say, I couldn't sleep. I see it as proof of my attachment to you."

Lucille found the two lovers dancing cheek to cheek to romantic music. Seeing them through the window of the front door, she paused before entering; the scene filled her with happiness. Robert and Martha's love was an answer to her prayers. She knew they wouldn't be married for a year or two, but she would have a daughter to love, and they wouldn't worry about her when they learned of her own plans.

She alone knew Gisèle's secret: she had accepted Lucille's invitation, and as soon as Philippe Beaudoin was released, he was going back to Gisèle. She had left Manitoba, but Manitoba had followed her. She was counting the days until her return. It would be a surprise for Martha and Robert.

Author BIO

Annette Saint-Pierre

Born in Quebec, Annette Saint-Pierre attended la Université d'Ottawa, completing her Ph.D. in 1979. She has been a teacher/administrator in rural Manitoba schools; Professor of French Canadian Literature a le Collége Universitaire de Saint-Boniface; and, since 1979, co-founder and managing editor of les Editions des Plaines. She has written novels, young adult fiction, historical essays, criticism and biography. She has contributed articles on many aspects of Franco-Manitoban life, participated in workshops, interviews and radio and television broadcasts on the same themes. She continues to focus on fiction, cultural history and theatre in Manitoba, especially as they pertain to Francophone life in Western Canada.

Translators BIO

André de Repentigny

André was born on February 23, 1942, in Montréal, Québec, where he has spent most of his life. He received his first education (elementary and high school) in French, and then he enrolled in a Bachelor of Arts degree program (Social Science) at Sir George Williams College (Concordia University).

While serving as a social worker in the City of Montréal's employ (a job he held for 18 years), he resumed his studies and earned a Bachelor's degree in Translation (English to French, and French to English) from Concordia University.

In 1995, he retired from the City of Montréal after 28 years of service, having worked, in the latter years, in his capacity as a translator, editor and writer.
In 2000, he got a Master's degree in Translation (French-to-English Literary Translation) from Université de Montréal.

From 2000 to 2003, André made Manitoba his home and worked for the Translation Services of the Province.

Now semi retired and living in Armagh, Québec, he works freelance from home and is always happy to be offered the opportunity to get involved in a literary translation project.

Béatrice Tellier

Born in St. Boniface, Manitoba, Béatrice was schooled at the Académie St-Joseph and Collège universitaire de St-Boniface. She then went on to obtain her Bachelor's degree of Education at the University of Manitoba and a licence en lettres, Université Aix-en-Provence, Balsac France. Shortly afterwards, Béatrice obtained a degree in music (piano), from the University of Toronto.

She has taught French and English in Manitoba, Ghana, Botswana and Alberta, mainly in Calgary. Following her sabbatical in Spain, she taught Spanish in Calgary. While in Fort McMurray, she edited a francophone newsletter and was organist at her church.

Beatrice has two adult children and has retired in Victoria.